T0090426

ALSO BY YVONNE BLACKWOOD

Into Africa a Personal Journey

Will That be Cash or 'Cuffs?

INTO AFRICA: THE RETURN

Yvonne Blackwood

Order this book online at www.trafford.com
or email orders@trafford.com

Most Trafford titles are also available at major online book retailers.

Printed in Victoria, BC, Canada.

ISBN: 978-1-4269-0265-9 (Soft)
ISBN: 978-1-4269-0267-3 (e-book)

We at Trafford believe that it is the responsibility of us all, as both individuals and corporations, to make choices that are environmentally and socially sound. You, in turn, are supporting this responsible conduct each time you purchase a Trafford book, or make use of our publishing services. To find out how you are helping, please visit www.trafford.com/responsiblepublishing.html

Our mission is to efficiently provide the world's finest, most comprehensive book publishing service, enabling every author to experience success. To find out how to publish your book, your way, and have it available worldwide, visit us online at www.trafford.com

Trafford rev. 11/09/2009

www.trafford.com

North America & international
toll-free: 1 888 232 4444 (USA & Canada)
phone: 250 383 6864 • fax: 812 355 4082 • email: info@trafford.com

DEDICATION

To dear cousin Pauline.

We shared an amazing grandmother who left us with incredible memories. Going on this journey together was delightful.

To my grandchildren Eliza and Monroe, always remember the African side of your ancestors.

"There is no greater sorrow on earth
than the loss of one's native land."

~Euripides 431 BC

AUTHOR'S NOTE

This travel memoir is a work of creative non-fiction. In 2000 my first book, *Into Africa: a personal journey,* was published. It was a bold response to the encouragement I had received from friends insisting that I share with the world the intriguing story of my journey to West Africa. The process propelled me into adding a new direction to my life – that of being an author. It also lit a fire in my American cousin, Peabody. She requested that I accompany her to Africa because the book and response to it had convinced her that she must visit this land of our ancestors, a place she had never thought of visiting. I agreed to return to Africa five years after the first journey. This book, *Into Africa: the Return,* articulates our experiences, and shares the joys, wonderment and sometimes sadness on the second journey.

In order to provide anonymity for some of the characters who are still living, several names have been changed. This book is, however, a true story based on my personal experience of a second fascinating journey to West Africa. The views and opinions expressed are my own originating from observation, conversations, notes, photographs, memory and research. No doubt other views and opinions exist about some events and places.

A big thank you to everyone who assisted me with this publication. A special thanks to Shadonna Richards for her valuable input, to Helen Sheppard for editing a few chapters and to Yvonne Komlenovich for her earlier input. A big thank you to editor, Sharon Crawford for her invaluable editing skills. I am deeply grateful to Cousin Peabody for taking up the challenge to finally visit Africa and for requesting my company. The exposure and experience the second time around still has me in a daze!

PROLOGUE

In 1997 I embarked on my first journey to the continent of Africa. I visited Ghana and Nigeria. The desire to visit the continent was spawn from a seed sown by my grandmother when I was a small child growing up in Jamaica. In the 1950s, we had no television. Our Sunday afternoon entertainment was storytelling. Grandmother was an excellent storyteller. The grandchildren would gather around her after dinner to listen to her amazing tales. A story told about my great-great grandfather mentioned that he used to say he was an Ashanti. He had garnered that information from his grandmother who came directly from Africa.

It is incredible how simple things can affect young impressionable minds; that story remained embedded in my head. Years later, I learned that Ashanti was a tribe in Ghana, West Africa and I began to develop an obsession to see that land. But the media was a great deterrent. Reports about Africa were always negative – war, fighting, disease, starvation. I became paralyzed with fear.

In 1997, I decided that come hell or high water, I would make the trip that year. I left Toronto during one of the coldest winters in fifty years to fulfill the quest. Preparation was sadly lacking. I had not received any inoculation, I knew no one in Ghana and I had no visa for Nigeria although I planned to spend a couple of weeks there with my sister-in-law. I travelled alone.

The journey was an intriguing one and after sharing some of the anecdotes with friends upon my return to Canada, they encouraged me to share the story with a wider audience - to write a book. The book *Into Africa a Personal Journey* vividly articulated my experiences. In it I shared my fears and trepidation, my excitement and joys, but most importantly, the kindness of the African men I encountered and of course the story about Adamson who gave me his love.

Five years after that fascinating experience, I returned to West

Africa, this time to Ghana and Togo. But this journey was quite different. A new dynamic was added – two American cousins, Peabody 70 and Marie 42 came along for the ride. And what a ride it was!

Peabody, a world-traveller, had refused to visit Africa over the years and had nothing positive to say about the land of our ancestors. It was a 360 degree turn-a-round when she decided to go on the journey and asked that I accompany her. She planned to spend a part of the time with Afua, her Ghanaian friend. Afua had invited her to visit Ghana many times but she had never accepted those invitations. The two had not seen each other for 40 years.

But Peabody wasn't the only one with great expectations. I had been sponsoring a young Ghanaian girl for a year; I would meet her and her pastor for the first time.

A big surprise awaited us. How we dealt with it, the fascinating places we visited, including one unscheduled country, is packaged into this amazing story, *Into Africa: The Return.*

Table of Contents

Dedication		v
Author's Note		vii
Prologue		ix
Chapter One	The Canopy Walk	1
Chapter Two	Adamson	9
Chapter Three	Peabody	16
Chapter Four	The Arrival	20
Chapter Five	Road to Kumasi	29
Chapter Six	Afua – Ashanti Woman	37
Chapter Seven	Ashanti Death	47
Chapter Eight	Sights and Sounds of Ghana	53
Chapter Nine	Road Trip to Cape Coast	70
Chapter Ten	Cape Coast Slave Castle	77
Chapter Eleven	The Dungeon	82
Chapter Twelve	Night on the Town	87
Chapter Thirteen	You Can't Go Back	95
Chapter Fourteen	The Preacher Man	99
Chapter Fifteen	Tema	104
Chapter Sixteen	Frieda	109
Chapter Seventeen	Road to Togo	117
Chapter Eighteen	Togo's Africa Gin	126
Chapter Nineteen	The Driver from Hell	134
Chapter Twenty	Logba Tota	139
Chapter Twenty-One	Tafi Atome	150
Chapter Twenty-Two	Return to Accra	154
Chapter Twenty-Three	Books for Frieda	156
Index		163

ONE

THE CANOPY WALK

WITH EVERY step I took, the narrow rope bridge rocked and swayed like an empty hammock on the beach being pummelled by the west wind. It creaked like an old wooden ship on the verge of falling apart. Then it hit me. I was suspended 30 metres in midair, high above the thick, lush rain forest in Ghana, supported by merely a network of ropes and cables, and a narrow 30-centimetre board, with slender metal bars on either side, used as a footpath. I wobbled in the middle of the first of seven stages of the bridge with no one to hold on to and no one to share my anxieties. The bridge was 350 metres long.

I had no concept of distance at this point. Then from the recesses of my mind, I recalled a fragment of sports trivia that a football field is about 109 metres long. It meant that the bridge where I stood was longer than three football fields put together! My salivary glands dried up instantly. My throat began to constrict. I became paralyzed.

After a few moments, I summoned up enough courage to continue the tortuous walk, staggering along the walkway as if intoxicated. My heart began to pound like a Kpanlogo drum and my body heated up far beyond the normal 37 degrees Celsius. My sweat glands, which had been inactive for a while, exploded and perspiration streamed down my face and back. I held a large white handkerchief in my right hand. It was a good time to blot the moisture, but I had pressed it unalterably against the rope and dared not let go to wipe my face. The sweat continued to flow. It dripped into my eyes and onto my lips.

At the beginning of the walk I had tucked my handbag tightly under my arm, straps over my shoulders, like a skydiver hooked up to a parachute. Gripping the ropes on either side of the narrow bridge, I kept going, knowing that my life depended on its support. I continued to put one heavy unsure foot in front of the other, slowly, and with calculation.

Then I felt another panic attack surging to the surface and the dryness in my throat intensified tenfold. I had six and a half more stages of the bridge to complete. It seemed the walk would take me forever. I now had a strong sense that primates and other wild creatures were waiting longingly beneath the deceptive canopy of shrubbery for lunch — my head, my limbs and my organs!

Dear God, what have I done?

My legs became weaker and weaker. I was breathing in spurts, my heart now racing faster than a cheetah rushing at its prey. How did I get myself into this mess? I CANNOT do this. I can't go any farther; I must go back.

The words of our guide roared inside my head. "If you're afraid of heights, don't look down; just look straight ahead." At that moment the bridge creaked louder than I'd heard it before and it swayed wider than it had ever done.

Oh God, I'm done for now!

I clung tighter to both sides of the thick rope bridge until my knuckles hurt. I wanted to cry, to pee, to do anything that would relieve the tension, anything to eradicate the nightmare, anything except to be on the bridge. I didn't look down; I couldn't even if I'd wanted to.

I decided then, that I wouldn't suffer anymore; I would swivel around and retrace my steps, not an easy movement on a narrow bridge that swayed constantly. It would be like turning on a dime, so to speak.

Gripping the ropes, I twisted my head slightly to glance at where I'd started this crazy, daring feat. To my horror, my cousin Marie, a heavy-set, 42-year-old woman, was already on the bridge, walking precariously toward me! That explained the wider sways and louder creaks.

Damn, I'm screwed.

I had Hobson's choice now; I could either leave or continue. Choice number one was not an option; there was no getting off, unless I wanted to fulfill the zestful desires of the ferocious animals waiting, lurking beneath the bushes.

Going back was out of the question too. Something else the guide had said flooded into my head. "Only one person is allowed on the bridge at a time." The person ahead of me would've completed stage one and moved onto the second leg by now. In another few moments, Marie would arrive at my spot and another person would step onto the bridge. With only four members of the group ahead of me, and Marie behind me, six tourists and two guides were still waiting to get on. I couldn't ruin this once-in-a lifetime adventure for the rest of the group. I had to move forward.

As I thought more about the situation, my fear changed to anger.

Wait until I see Charles Ansah again; if I ever do, I'll strangle him with my bare hands! He got me into this.

The previous day I'd told Charles that my cousins and I planned to spend two days in Cape Coast, the main reason being to visit the famous Elmina and Cape Coast slave castles.

"You're planning to spend only two days here?" Charles had asked, his voice tempered with disappointment.

"Yes, our friend from Kumasi told us there wasn't much to see in Cape Coast except the slave castles."

"She doesn't know what she's talking about." His strong African voice exhibited annoyance and so did the expression on his face. "There's a lot to see here. One place you must see is Kakum National Park, and you have to go on the Canopy Walkway."

"The Canopy Walkway? What is that? I've never heard about it before."

"Really? It's world famous. The park opened officially in 1994 but the Canopy Walkway was completed in 1997."

"That explains why I hadn't heard of it then; it was probably not completed when I arrived in Ghana last time."

"It's the only rainforest walkway in Africa. That place is a major tourist destination and attracts more tourists now than almost anything else in Ghana."

Pride exuded from his face, pride that his part of the country was bringing in well-needed foreign exchange. I was taken aback to hear about the place as I'd not done so on my first visit to Ghana. That shouldn't surprise me, because I was quite uninformed at that time and hadn't done any research. Back then I was merely obsessed with seeing the land of my ancestors. Now that my curiosity had been appeased, I was deeply interested in Ghana's culture and history. Charles seemed eager to show off Kakum National Park and because my cousins, Peabody and Marie, who were travelling with me, wanted to see and learn as much as they could about Ghana, we agreed to visit it.

That Tuesday morning the sky looked like a mural on an artist's canvas: cotton-candy white clouds rested uniformly across a clear blue sky. The African sun bathed Cape Coast like a soothing balm. After a late breakfast, my cousins and I piled into Charles's Opel and headed out, excited to see the famous place. Two kilometres outside of the village of Abrafo, we arrived at the main pavilion of Kakum National Park. Charles informed us that he would not accompany us on the hike or the canopy walk but he would be waiting to pick us up when we returned. I didn't think anything of it, assuming he'd done the tour so many times, he would find it boring. We signed up and paid 60,000 cedis each to join the next tour. It was scheduled to begin in an hour, so we decided to kill time by visiting the small museum located in the complex. Charles accompanied us. The museum, well-organized and documented, featured several plants with rich medicinal values and animals that inhabited the rain forest. At the beginning of the tour, I tapped Peabody on the shoulder.

"Hey P, did you see the quotation over there?" I nodded toward the centre of the room.

"What quotation?" She strained her eyes, staring through her glasses to see.

"There's a little plaque on the wall over there; you see it? It's a quotation by Ade Nyinaa Dan Suahi. It says 'All knowledge is acquired by experience.' "

"Isn't that the truth," Peabody said.

"And here we are acquiring some."

"Yes, you ladies will learn a lot today," Charles said from behind us.

The hour flew by and soon a group gathered to listen to instructions from Robert, our tour guide for the hike and canopy walk. Following closely behind Robert, we climbed a steep hill, 335 metres above sea level, walking on solid rock as we ascended into Kakum's rain forest. When we arrived at the top, I held my head down, my chin almost touching my knees, as I huffed and puffed like a tired steam engine, and tried to channel air back into my lungs. Sweat oozed from every pore and streamed down my face. The large handkerchief I had been using to wipe my face was completely saturated. Using both hands, I wrung it as if it were laundry, flapped it in the wind to release the wrinkles, then wiped my face again.

Robert was medium built, about twenty-four, and dressed in a crisp khaki suit. He stood facing the group, surrounded by tall trees that partially blocked out the sunlight, as he gave us a well-rehearsed overview of the rain forest.

"This part of the forest consists of 360 square kilometres and is conserved with the agreement and help of the Ghanaian government and some world organizations. There are over 40 species of large mammals such as elephants and Royal antelopes in this forest. There are over 300 different species of birds, 400 species of butterflies and hundreds of insects. There are also reptiles."

Peabody shivered and looked around with wide bulging eyes. She hates reptiles.

"Don't worry P, I'm sure you won't come close to any," I whispered and squeezed her hand.

"There are more than 200 species of plants per square hectare," Robert said. "Some of the trees in the forest are over 60 metres high. Most of the animals in this forest are nocturnal so I can't guarantee that you'll see any today. But don't worry; they already know you're here; some can pick up your scent two kilometres away. Any questions?"

An uneasy feeling crept over me. Hungry wild beasts were watching us but we couldn't see them! Robert gave us more information and told us about the canopy walkway. I listened attentively at first, then tuned out. He surveyed the group. There were six Caucasians (four Swedish girls in their teens and a middle-aged Dutch couple), three virile, black American men (they were old friends born in Jamaica, but all had immigrated to the United States many years ago) Peabody, Marie and me. Robert was the main guide and Sam, no more than 18 years, was his assistant. No one posed a question, so Robert continued.

"Please do not disturb the animals by making too much noise. Do not disturb the plants by stepping on the roots or by shaking the branches. Many of the plants in this forest have valuable medicinal value. Some are used to make soaps, perfumes, and of course, drugs."

We moved on, walking single file behind Robert, into the heart of the forest. Along the way, Robert pointed out several trees and gave details about them. At one spot we came upon a huge tree trunk in our path.

"This trunk has been lying here for more than 10 years," Robert said.

Several strange insects were crawling across the log.

"Do you see these insects? They actually have a hundred legs, which is why they're called centipedes."

"How did this huge log get here?" one of the Swedish girls asked. It was an interesting question; the log seemed so out of place.

"Logging was big business in this forest at one time and a logging company chopped down this tree. But when they realized that it was impossible to transport such a large tree out of the forest, they left it here."

We continued until we reached the entrance to the world-renowned Canopy Walkway. Robert stopped to explain the rules before we were allowed on.

"The canopy walkway bridge is 350 metres long and is suspended 30 metres above the forest. It is divided into seven sections and has six platforms. Only one person is allowed on each section at a time. Once you reach the mid-point of a bridge section, another person can start walking. You can only go one way. The bridge will sway while you're on and it will creak, but don't worry, it is safe."

"Any one ever fall off?" the Dutch man asked and laughed nervously, exposing cigarette-stained teeth. I visualized him seeing someone scared to death, tumbling off.

"Not that I know of."

I hardly think he would divulge that information, you blockhead.

"The oldest woman to do this walk was 87 years old and the oldest man was 96," said Robert. "He was an ex-service man from England."

I digested the guide's words. A piece of cake! How high could 30 metres be? And 350 metres, that couldn't be all that long, could it? Born and raised in Jamaica, a former British colony, I'd grown up using the British measurement system and therefore thought in terms of inches and yards. I'm still unable to do a mental calculation to convert to metric, so 350 metres didn't mean anything to me. But what the heck? I was ready for the adventure.

"Who will go on first?" Robert asked. He scrutinized the group, a challenging look on his face.

Two of the black American men decided to exhibit their "machomanship" and volunteered to begin the walk. Cousin Peabody piped up that she would be third. The other American said he would be fourth. I quickly volunteered to take spot number five. I didn't want to be first but most certainly didn't want to be last either. Marie opted for spot number six and so the adventure began.

In the middle of my panic attack, I remembered dear cousin Peabody. I love her greatly; she's like the big sister I never had, but she was becoming a major challenge and I was pissed. I hadn't seen her huff and puff to climb the hill into the forest as I had; in fact, unlike me, she was composed and breathing normally when we reached the top. Peabody was Marie's mother and 70 years old. How could I allow a woman 18 years my senior, a retiree now privileged with senior's discounts, the satisfaction of being braver than I? There was no way. If she could accomplish this feat, walk 350 metres on a swaying, creaking rickety bridge, so could I. Envisioning the taunting I would receive if I chickened out strengthened my resolve. I thought about Marie heading my way, and of the other eight people behind, waiting anxiously to begin the daring walk. What kind of message would I send them if I backed out? What kind of respect would I receive if I showed cowardice now? I would ruin everything for them. Besides, I was a strong woman, a banker accustomed to making tough decisions, and a mentor of black youths who looked up to me. No, despite my fear and trepidation, I had to go through with it. I took several deep breaths, whispered a prayer, mustered up every ounce of courage in my being, and kept on going, hanging onto the ropes as the bridge continued its spineless dance. The boards creaked and groaned, and in the quietness of the rainforest with only the chirping of birds, the creaking was magnified many times. I placed my belief in, and focused on the words of the guide, "Don't worry; it is safe."

Exotic butterflies flitted by, butterflies one could only imagine based on illustrations in fairytale books. One, as white as new fallen snow, whizzed passed my head. I wanted to gaze at it, to stretch out my hand to it, but I didn't have the nerve to turn my head to admire it or to let go even one hand to beckon to it. The rope bridge in the Indiana Jones movie, *Raiders of the Lost Ark*, paled in comparison to this one. Finally, I consoled myself that others had done the walk before me and had survived. Didn't Robert say a 96-year-old man had done it? Why would the good Lord choose my turn to snap the bridge?

Bearing that in mind, I plodded on and on, looking straight

ahead until I came upon the first platform. At the end of each section of the bridge, platforms were firmly anchored to giant trees 100 to 400 years old. I stepped off the bridge, stood on the first platform, and exhaled.

It was only here that I had the confidence to look down and over the forest for the first time. A panorama of magnificent emerald foliage unfolded before my eyes. The view was spectacular. Such a view could not be seen from the ground. The flora was a canopy of trees of varying sizes, ages and colour spectrum, all competing fiercely for the sunlight and the rain. Everything seemed so organized, so meticulously planned. It was Mother Nature at her best and I marvelled at the power of the Creator.

Soon I stepped onto the second bridge and continued the walk, gaining more confidence as it swayed and creaked, but never looking down until I placed my feet onto the other platforms. There I took it all in like a drug, then moved on.

I was one-third the distance of the final stretch of the seventh bridge when I looked straight ahead and saw Peabody and the three black Americans standing under a small covered platform. They had completed the walk and had positioned themselves to cheer the rest of the group along. I grinned from ear to ear and knew there would be no turning back for me; the mission would be accomplished; I would complete the entire walk.

Out of the tranquility, and without any warning, a booming clap of thunder rocked the forest. It scared me so; I jumped and almost fell off the bridge. Raindrops, the size of ping-pong balls fell intermittently and splattered on my head and arms.

No, it can't be. It can't rain now. I'm still on the bridge!

Then it dawned on me; we're in the middle of a rain forest. It meant expect rain at anytime. Thunder boomed again, this time louder, and it rolled on a continuum, one roll culminating in another and another. Prongs of lightning pierced the forest, illuminating it as if providing light for some unseen beings. In the middle of the rumble and flashes of lightning, like a fireworks display, the heavens opened and rain began to pour. . . .

TWO

ADAMSON

WITH GIGANTIC raindrops pounding on my head and face, I burst into laughter that only a hyena could outdo. Adding pep to my steps, I gripped the rope more tightly and kept moving. Moments later, I crossed the finish line and ran into Peabody's arms. We embraced and kissed. The three American men rushed to hug me.

"All right, Sister, you did it," one said.

"Congrats," another chimed in.

"That was some thrill," I said feebly. I had a lot more to say, but those were the only words that I could express at that moment.

I had an eerie sense of karma, the kind that one experiences after a highly-charged emotional episode ends well. Once the feeling of "I can't do anything more; I can't stand it another minute," dissipates, you can see the proverbial light at the end of the tunnel and your soul reacts. It's over. I've conquered. I've won. I felt victorious and elated.

The five of us waited under the covered platform for the rest of the group to complete the walk. Rain continued to pour mercilessly and water began to drip through the roof. I was wet, but the rest who came after were soaked. When Richard arrived, his crisp khaki suit had lost its shade; it was now a dark chocolate colour and it clung to him like a wet t-shirt on a model. The last person and Sam, the assistant guide, arrived 30 minutes after I'd completed the walk. I felt sorry for them. The woman had to remove her outer garments and wring them to remove some of the moisture.

We waited on the platform for another 15 minutes but the rain continued unabated. The thunder never stopped rolling and lightning flashed intermittently.

"Do you think it will stop soon?" The Dutchman asked Robert.

"Sometimes it stops almost as soon as it starts, but sometimes it can rain for a long time."

I hope this is not one of the long times.

It was raining less and slower but it wouldn't end. Some members of the group decided that they wouldn't wait any longer and started climbing down the steep hill to return to the pavilion where we began the trek. My cousins and I joined them. I was concerned that Charles might have returned for us and was probably worried about our non-appearance.

Slowly and carefully we descended the hill. The rocks were wet and slippery. When we reached the café we were soaked to our undies.

So how did I find myself on such a wild emotional roller coaster? How did a 52-year-old Canadian citizen of Jamaican heritage with bad knees and a sore hip end up first on a tottering rope bridge across the Ghanaian rain forest and then sopping wet to her underwear? Ghana wasn't a major tourist destination. Why was I there in the first place? Was it a death wish? Was I a wild daredevil who craved excitement? The answer to the latter two questions is a resounding NO.

I mentioned earlier that Charles Ansah had recommended the canopy walkway, but the journey to Africa had its incubation many years before he came into the picture. To put this incredible story in a proper sequence, I must take you back to the beginning or close to it . . . .

. . . . Adamson is dead.

The mere thought of putting the words in black and white caused chills to run up and down my spine. It transformed a situation from several years of surrealism into reality. I wasn't sure that I wanted it to be so. The lean, lanky Ghanaian Adonis and I had become fast friends during my first visit to his country. With enthusiasm and effervescence, Adamson had helped me to experience the sights and sounds of Ghana. He'd been my tour guide, driver, companion, doctor, and more. Now he was gone. So many times I've thought about him, wishing circumstances were different, and would give anything to turn back the hands of time. But I could do nothing to reconstruct the path. It was history.

The day I heard the news has remained in my memory as fresh as a cool wind off the Matterhorn. One freezing cold February morning I was sitting in my office with eyes glued to the computer screen, editing a report I had typed. I looked up, merely to give my eyes a rest, and saw fluffy white snowflakes cascading past the wide floor-to-ceiling window and landing on the pavement. Despite living for more than a quarter of a century in Canada, I'd never grown fond of snow. Mind you, I can appreciate a gentle snowfall that barely changes the colour of the sidewalk, and I like to admire it powdering the evergreens. At Christmas time I enjoy watching it glisten on the pine and spruce trees, but I much prefer to observe heavy snowfalls from the comfort of my home. Slipping and sliding in it had never excited me. Since I didn't plan to leave the office for several hours, I ignored the precipitation and continued to edit the report.

I had just changed a "there" to "their" on page six when the phone rang. I snatched it from the cradle.

"May I speak to Miss Blackwood?" an unfamiliar voice asked.

"You are speaking to her."

"This is Norman Osuno calling. Remember me? We met several months ago."

I remembered him immediately. His Ghanaian accent was very distinct and as there weren't many Ghanaians telephoning me, the voice was easy to figure out. He was a friend of Adamson's sister and a businessman who owned a used clothing company in Toronto. Adamson had been desperate to immigrate to Canada after we'd met, and realizing it would be difficult to do so on his own, he'd tried to arrange a sponsor. Two years after I returned from Africa, he'd asked me to meet and plead with Norman Osuno to encourage him to be a sponsor. I'd reluctantly telephoned Norman and he'd invited me to visit him at his office to discuss the matter. He greeted me warmly and took me on a brief tour of his company.

"I have 30 people working for me," he said as we moved along mounds of clothing.

"So where do you export all these clothes to?"

"Mainly Africa, Ghana naturally, Zaire and Bangladesh also."

Several young ladies worked in the factory. They separated clothes and tossed them onto different piles.

"What are the different categories for sorting?"

"Well, we have piles for children, men, women, whites, and rags. It really depends on what we get in." He showed me a large machine. "See this? This machine wraps and bundles the clothes before we ship them."

"I had no idea about this kind of business." The sheer volume fascinated me.

"It's a good business. There are a few people doing it, mainly East Indians."

After the tour we returned to Norman's office and his secretary brought us cold drinks. The factory was like an oven. It lacked air-conditioning; just a few ceiling fans swished overhead. A cold drink was just what I needed. I leaned back in a chair facing Norman's desk and drank mine gratefully.

"So your friend wants to immigrate here?"

"Yes, he's desperate."

Norman looked at me with raised brows, and I knew he thought I was the instigator.

I laughed. "I assure you, it's without encouragement from me. I've tried to explain to Adamson that it isn't easy for a guy like him, with no assets and no licensed skills, to get approval to immigrate to Canada."

"I know the sister well and I would like to help but it can't be now. I have two nephews in Ghana and they want to come here too. I must attend to them first."

"Look, Norman, I fully understand; blood is thicker than water."

"Tell your friend he is looking at about a two-year wait before I can even begin to help him."

"I will. Thanks for taking the time to consider it."

Later that night, I telephoned Adamson and relayed the information.

He was extremely upset. "What am I going to do? Are yuh going to let me die here?" he asked bitterly.

"Adamson, don't be ridiculous. What do you mean die? You are a young, healthy man with your whole life ahead of you. It's not the end of the world. Maybe you're not meant to travel to North America just yet. And anyway, two years is not a long time. Try to work hard and save as much money as you can in the meantime." I tried to console him but I could sense his frustration and disappointment.

Now realizing the voice on the line was that of Adamson's potential sponsor, I was all ears.

"Hello Norman, so nice to hear from you."

My thoughts raced. Maybe he'd changed his mind. Could it be that he was going to sponsor Adamson right away? Or maybe he had an even better suggestion.

"Are you sitting down?" he asked.

"Yes, I'm at my desk," I replied cheerfully. The proverbial meaning of such a question flew right over my head.

"I'm afraid I have some bad news for you." He hesitated as if trying to put his words together.

I sighed, figuring he wasn't going to sponsor Adamson after all.

"Just a minute, let me close my door."

My office was located in a busy bank branch. The chatter of customers and staff and the whirl of machines flooded through the open door. Sometimes it became so noisy, it drowned out voices on my telephone. I put Norman on hold and quickly closed the door. Returning to my chair, I picked up the instrument, not knowing what to expect.

"Yes, what is it?"

"I'm calling to tell you that your friend Adamson passed away."

My heart stopped beating and my body became numb, dead to all sensations. I'm not sure how many seconds passed; it seemed like minutes; maybe it was minutes; then in a haze I heard Norman's voice.

"Miss Blackwood. Hello Miss Blackwood! Are you there? Did you hear what I said?"

Life began to seep back into to my limbs. "I'm here. Did you say Adamson is dead? How?" I had a hundred more questions requiring answers but I couldn't think fast enough.

"They say he was brushing his teeth one morning and he fell down. He had a massive heart attack. He died almost instantly."

My head began to whirl. My poor, dear Adamson. I wanted to see him, to talk to him. It couldn't be true.

On a quest to fulfill a life-long dream to see the land of my ancestors, I'd visited Ghana and Nigeria in 1997. The desire for that came from a story my grandmother had told me. My mother's parents had raised me in rural Jamaica, since age two and a half, when my mother had died. That was in the 1950s; we were poor and had only a radio and gramophone for entertainment. Television arrived in the area in the early '60s, and even by then we couldn't afford one. Storytelling became a major form of entertainment. When Grandmother Eliza told the story that her grandfather, when angry, used to yell "I'm Ashanti!"

a seed was sown. Great great-grandfather had obtained that information from his grandmother who came directly from Africa. Years later I learned that Ashanti was a tribe in Ghana, West Africa and from then I developed an obsession to see that place.

On my first visit to Africa I'd spent eight days in Adamson's country and all during those wonderful days we'd been together constantly. My mind flashed back to several special moments with him: the time we had dined at a small restaurant with red and white checkerboard table cloths, when he'd shown me how to eat fufu and the disappointed look on his face when I was unable to swallow it. In his delicious accent he'd asked, accusingly, "So yuh don't like my fufu?" Another day he'd taken me to meet his family, and to see where he lived. His little nieces and nephews, excited to see a foreign visitor, whispered about me in their dialect. I'd asked him what they were saying and he said they wanted to know if he was going to marry me! Then there was the Sunday afternoon we'd spent at Labadi Beach listening to drummers, watching dancers and drinking Star beer. But the most vivid recollection was our trip to Kumasi and the night we'd spent together. I'd caught a nasty cold, probably from travelling dusty roads. As chills racked my body, he'd wrapped his arms around me and I'd curled up against him in the Stadium Hotel, trying to get his body warmth to take away the chill. It was then he'd declared his love for me. I'd fluffed it off, insisting it was infatuation but we'd kept in touch during the next three years. Maybe it was love. Whatever it was, he had never wavered. He'd kept me up to date on the goings-on in his life – his father had died and one of his sisters had given birth to another child. I'd kept all his cards, letters and photographs stashed neatly in a bottom drawer of my dresser.

I didn't want to hear what Norman was saying. I suddenly remembered that he was still on the telephone and pulled myself together.

"When did this happen? When is the funeral?"

"He died a week ago. As you know, Muslims don't keep dead bodies long; he's already buried."

Like driving the last nail into a wooden box, like licking and sealing an envelope, the job was finished; it all sounded so final. Adamson and I had spoken on the phone only a week earlier. He must have died shortly after.

"Thank you so much for calling me and giving me the information. There was a reason why we met. Had it not been for you I probably would never have known. I would love to send condolences to his mother. Can you get me the mailing address?"

I didn't have Adamson's home address as he'd always used a post box for our correspondence.

"Sure. I'll call the sister. She's the one who told me about the death. I'm sorry to have to give you this news." Norman rang off.

I sat at my desk for almost an hour, stunned. I couldn't think, couldn't concentrate, couldn't work. The report would just have to wait. Images of the six-foot-six Ghanaian with the broad wide grin darted through my mind over and over again. I recalled his voice, deep and sensuous, his words, how he habitually added "Dat is all" at the end of his sentences, and I remembered his touch. How could this be? Why had fate dealt him such a cruel hand? I tried to cry – I wanted to – but not a single tear came to my eyes; my tear glands were frozen. A splitting ache crept across my forehead. Shortly after, I left work for the rest of the day.

Two and a half years after Adamson's death, and five years after my first visit to the continent, I was on my way to Africa for the second time. My first visit lacked preparation; at the time I was simply filled with an obsession to see Africa. This time I was prepared. Visas for Ghana and Mali were stamped indubitably in my passport. I'd received shots for yellow fever weeks in advance, and I'd swallowed my first malaria pill a week earlier. I intended to follow my doctor's instructions to, "Take one Lariam once per week on the same day while you are in Africa and continue to take them when you return until you've taken all eight pills."

Yes, I had taken all necessary precautions; I wouldn't have to drive myself crazy, hoping and praying that I didn't catch a tropical disease as I'd done on my first visit. But I knew one thing for certain; the experience would never be the same as the first, for as the saying goes, lightning never strikes in the same place twice. The experience five years previously, was too unique, too spiritual, to be repeated. For one thing, this time I wasn't travelling alone; Peabody and Marie were with me. Also, there would be no Adamson. Would I re-connect with any of the other wonderful, kind men I'd encountered on my first visit? Would I find another Adamson? What would I discover this time? Maybe lightening could actually strike twice. Only time would tell.

THREE

PEABODY

PEABODY IS the daughter of my mother's only sister, making us first cousins. We were raised in Jamaica by the same grandmother and shared her boundless, unconditional love. Peabody, 18 years older than I, had the opportunity to know our great-great grandfather, but he died before I was born. She remembers him vividly and describes him as a short, very dark-skinned man who stuttered and loved to remind anyone who crossed him that, "I . . . I'm. . . Ashanti!"

But besides that minute hint that our ancestors came from Africa, that continent was never discussed or mentioned at home. As far as Peabody and I were concerned, we were British. Effigies of King George V1, and later Queen Elizabeth 11, were overtly imprinted on our money. Our currency was sterling – pounds, shillings and pence; our measurements were gallons, pints, yards and inches. We sang *God Save Our Gracious Queen* at school and at functions, and our flag was the Union Jack.

Jamaica gained her independence from Britain in 1962 and the citizens were introduced to a new flag. The currency changed to the Jamaican dollar and a new pride of freedom permeated the country.

In the early 1960s, Peabody immigrated to England. There she met and befriended a Ghanaian woman named Afua Bonsu. Afua was training as a nurse and succeeded in becoming one. Eventually she returned to Ghana while Peabody immigrated to the United States. They corresponded for over forty years. Afua invited Peabody many times to visit her in Ghana but she never accepted the offer. It seems Afua finally gave up on her friend, because although they kept in touch, the invitation was never mentioned in later years.

Peabody loved to travel and visited many countries all over the world, but confessed that she'd never had a desire to visit Africa. Wherever she travelled, she always took the time to learn a few popular phrases in each country's language. At one of our kitchen-table tête-à-têtes in Rochester, she shared this story with her daughters and me.

"I was in Moscow attending a church convention. You know how tight the schedule is for these things; you don't get any time to shop. Well, one day after one of the evening's events, two of the sisters and I slipped out of the hotel and went into town to do some shopping. I noticed a lovely babushka in a window and entered the store intending to buy it." At this point Peabody stood and demonstrated the action. "I greeted the clerk: 'Dobroye utro.' The woman looked at me wide-eyed, then burst into a big grin. She began to rattle off Russian at the rate of a hundred miles per minute. When she eventually calmed down, I tried to explain that I knew only a little bit of Russian. You should've seen the disappointment on her face; it was priceless."

At age 62, Peabody developed a severe case of diabetes. The disease attacked her with such fury, she lost her sight for six weeks. With the help of good doctors, she was fortunate to regain her sight. After that dramatic episode, she read extensively about the disease and worked closely with her doctors. She lost 50 pounds and became a model patient for diabetes. Peabody even appeared on TV where she shared her story. She continued to eat well, exercise daily, and today she's healthy and energetic. She monitors her blood sugar every day and has not allowed diabetes to limit her activities.

Unlike me, Peabody never yearned to visit Africa, the land of our ancestors. But it seems you can't avoid your destiny; sooner or later some things become totally out of your control because they are so ordained. After my first journey to West Africa in 1997, I shared my story and photographs with Peabody. It piqued her interest that perhaps she should visit Africa. When my book, *Into Africa a Personal Journey* was published, many of her friends purchased copies and their positive responses to the story reinforced the idea that she had missed a wonderful opportunity. She questioned herself: "Why had I visited all these 'white' countries and never given a thought to seeing the continent where my ancestors came from?"

One night, Peabody telephoned me from Rochester and made a request.

"Yvonne my dear, I want you to do me a favour."

Peabody rarely asks for favours; I was keen to hear the request.

"Yes Cuz, what can I do for you?"

"I would like to visit Ghana in two years time, but I want you to go with me. Will you do that?"

"Well, well, well, after all these years you want to go to Africa now?" I asked. I sensed her knowing smile through the phone.

"Yes. After reading your book, and hearing the reaction from friends who bought it, I think I should."

I was shocked. "Be honest with me P; tell me the real reason why you have never wanted to go before."

"Well, you know, you hear so much about violence over there. It makes me afraid."

I sharpened my tongue to give her a lecture that would put her straight for good, but realizing that she had made a decision to go, suggested that she had at least overcome some of her fears. Bearing that in mind, I kept it simple.

"My dear," I said. "From time immemorial, man has always been involved in war. Just read your Bible. Somewhere, at some corner of the globe, there is always war or political upheaval; the world is never at peace."

"I know; you're right," Peabody said.

I was thrilled that she had made such a monumental decision.

"Two years from now I should be able to save enough. As you know, I have a few other countries I would like to visit, but we'll work with it."

It was a promise she knew I would keep.

In 2002, before we embarked on the journey, the world had not changed. Taiwan, Israel, Venezuela, Pakistan and Afghanistan (to name a few) were experiencing major turmoil. The continent of Africa also had its fair share. In Sierra Leone, UNAMSIL disarmed tens of thousands of fighters who had fought on both sides of the country's civil war. More than 42,000 fighters handed in their weapons, paving the way for presidential and parliamentary elections. In Zimbabwe, the Sub-Saharan Africa Diplomatic Affairs (SADC) met in Malawi to discuss planned presidential elections, and President Robert Mugabe agreed to ensure fair elections. Sad to say, a month later, police charged Morgan Tsvangirai, the opposition leader, with treason, alleging that Tsvangiri was involved in a plot to assassinate Mugabe. Tsvangirai denied the charges – he was running for president against President Mugabe. In Angola, Jonas Savimbi, leader of the rebel National Union for Total Independence of Angola, was killed in a clash with government forces. In Algeria, Antar Zouabri, leader of the rebel Armed Islamic Group, was killed in a shootout with government forces. In the Democratic Republic of Congo, fighting occurred between ethnic Lendu and Hema militia in the northeast; and in the Ivory Coast, mutinous troops seized Bouake and Korhogo.

In the summer of 2002, Peabody and I discussed when and where we would visit. We decided on Ghana and Mali. Peabody telephoned Afua to give her the good news. She was overjoyed; her friend was finally coming to Ghana. One of Peabody's daughters, Marie, surprised her and stated that she wanted to go on the journey too. I made all the arrangements for the flight from Canada.

One cold day in October, Peabody and Marie packed their clothes, monitoring machine and medications and travelled to Toronto. They spent a night with me. The next day the three of us boarded an airplane bound for Amsterdam where we would take a connecting flight to Ghana.

FOUR

THE ARRIVAL

On a crisp, cold October morning, the KLM 747 taxied down the runway at Pearson International airport in Toronto. Unlike my first journey to Africa where I'd travelled alone, this time a new dynamic had been added; I was travelling with my cousins Peabody and Marie. It was their first pilgrimage to the Motherland. We sat together three in a row; I occupied the window seat, Peabody the middle, and Marie, a big girl who needed more room, sat in the aisle seat.

I looked out the small window, then closed my eyes. As I always did when I flew, I whispered a prayer that we would arrive at our destination safely. The aircraft lifted, then soared above the sprawling city that was just coming to life. As we levelled off at 35,000 feet, my thoughts brimmed over with one thing only – Adamson. All the wonderful memories I had of him passed through my mind like countryside sceneries from a moving train; a palette of colours, frame by frame, crammed with emotions and feelings. Without any warning, my eyes welled up; tears spilled forth, and flowed uncontrollably down my cheeks. It was the first time that I'd cried for him since his death. I kept my eyes glued to the nothingness beyond the small airplane window and wept silently. The gaping seam would be sewn up tightly; I knew it was the closure that I needed. I'd finally put Adamson to rest, but I would never forget him. I don't think Peabody was aware of my crying, but if she was, she never let on. Watching a jumble of clouds floating by, I made a concerted effort to put Adamson out of my mind; I decided to focus on Frieda instead.

The theory of "six degrees of separation" can be difficult to accept; however, after you've seen it in operation you become a believer quickly. I'd been a banker for most of my working life, but when I became an author, a fresh dimension was added to my existence. But it is the new connections and new friends made as a result that I find most rewarding. After my first book, *Into Africa a Personal Journey*, was published and doing well, I'd pledged to use some of the proceeds to assist at least one child in Ghana. At the time, I knew no one who could refer a child and I was leery of using organizations. I'd always felt (rightly or wrongly) that organizations spend too much of donated funds on administration and that not enough goes to the people donors want to help.

One day, my publisher forwarded to me an e-mail he'd received from a woman named Anita Sinclair. Anita wrote that she had read my book, loved it and was excited about it. She had recently returned from Ghana with a church group, was much enamoured with the country; she had also undergone some experiences similar to the ones mentioned in the book. She felt as if she knew me! Could we keep in touch? Thrilled with the reader's response, I replied to the e-mail. After that, Anita and I became great friends on the Internet. It is interesting how we draw conclusions and conjure up images of individuals we've never met when we merely correspond with them or speak to them on the telephone. I'd assumed that Anita was a black woman from Canada. After a few e-mails she sent me pictures of herself and family. It turned out she was a blue-eyed, platinum-blond, middle-aged woman from North Carolina. She gloated about two wonderful ministers she'd worked with in Tema, Ghana, and a bit about the community. Realizing that maybe the child I wanted to assist could be in that community, I asked Anita to investigate. I wanted to help either a boy or girl of high school age with their education, but preferably a girl.

It didn't take long. Anita responded, yes, there was a 12-year-old girl called Frieda. Her parents had recently separated and the mother was left to take care of the child. Frieda had attended a private school but her mother could no longer afford the fees. My wish was answered; Frieda became the chosen one. Anita connected me to Pastor Ray, the junior pastor of the church that Frieda attended, and sent me a photo of her. She was cute as a Barbie doll. Frieda and I began to communicate by letters and later via e-mail. She became my little protégée. On this trip, I would meet her for the first time.

Thinking about Frieda, I became both excited and curious. But before I met her, I would meet Pastor Ray, the minister who had recommended her. A bolt of nervousness jolted me. Pastor Ray and I had communicated by e-mail for a year and I'd sent funds directly to him for Frieda. His e-mail messages had been friendly and warm and always ended with "Be blessed." Strange, that as I thought about him, I wondered if he was anything like Adamson. I would have to wait and see, but I felt there could never be another Adamson.

It didn't matter how well you planned, when it came to travelling, you could never anticipate all the possible bumps in the road. The terrorist attack of 9/11 had also removed much of the fun from air travel. Our KLM flight was to take us to Amsterdam Airport Schiphol where we would stop over for seven hours, then connect to a direct flight to Ghana. We arrived in Amsterdam on schedule. We took the opportunity to explore the huge airport and bought food, souvenirs, and delectable Swiss chocolates.

Mother Nature had her own plan, one that no one could foretell, not even sophisticated weather bureaus. A freak snowstorm swept over Europe that day. Soon cancellation notices began to appear on the airport monitors. I had no concern because our flight to Accra, Ghana was scheduled for seven hours later. I assumed all would be in order by that time. Just before our flight was due to leave, the monitor showed that departure time had changed to 4:30 p.m.

Okay, an extra two hours wait. No problem.

But before then, our new departure time changed again to 6 p.m., then 8 p.m. Finally, at 12:15 a.m. it was cancelled.

After 17 hours we were still sitting on the tough black resin chairs with chrome armrests at Amsterdam Airport Schiphol. Thousands of other passengers were in the same predicament. No announcements were made; signs on the monitors just flashed *cancelled, cancelled, cancelled. . . .*

Hundreds of passengers, including my cousins and I, joined the transfer line in an attempt to change flights, cancel or book for the next available flight. Tempers flared and voices rose to a crescendo. At about 1 a.m., airline personnel handed out a few blankets and small foam pillows, but not enough for everyone. People slept on floors, some curled up in corners, some against walls or on the hard black chairs. At 1.30 a.m., the counter clerks stopped working and advised us to try again at six in the morning. They distributed form letters of explanation along with airmail letters to be used for complaints.

What good would a complaint letter do for us at a time like this? I suppose it's psychological warfare.

Half an hour later two KLM personnel arrived pushing trolleys loaded with more blankets and pillows. A very frustrated woman demanded a blanket immediately.

"You'll only get one if you ask for it nicely," one of the attendants said.

Such a bloody nerve.

I felt badly for Peabody and Marie, more than I did for myself. Here they were on their first journey to Africa only to have to endure such an awful experience. I had travelled the same route on my first journey and everything had gone without a snag. But I suppose we could blame the time of year. I'd travelled in January then; this time we were travelling in October.

We spent 48 hours at Amsterdam Airport Schiphol. We were able to purchase decent meals, but we were tired and dirty.

The 747 touched down at Kotoka International Airport in Ghana without a glitch. We cleared customs and immigration with ease. Putting the unfortunate experience at Amsterdam behind us, we tried to focus on the place we were enthusiastic to see. We exited the terminal building and found major construction underway. Because of this, relatives and friends who'd come to meet their loved ones had to wait outside near the parking lot. With our luggage in tow, we walked cautiously along a makeshift ramp. Peabody strained her eyes to try to spot our host, Afua. Although they'd kept in touch, they hadn't seen each other for 40 years; in essence Peabody wasn't sure what to expect.

At the end of the ramp a young man holding up a makeshift cardboard sign was almost run over by a returning Ghanaian woman with a huge suitcase.

Where on earth do they buy their suitcases? I didn't realize they make them that big.

The three of us read the inscription on the cardboard sign in unison.

"Peabody Tomlinson."

I had no idea how many Peabody Tomlinsons lived in Ghana, land of 20 million people (2003), or how many would've been returning home on the day we arrived, but we assumed it pertained to our Peabody.

We approached the young man.

"Are you here from Afua Bonsu?" Peabody asked.

"Yes, Mrs. Bonsu asked me to meet Peabody. You're Peabody?"

"Yes, I'm the one."

"I'm George, her nephew."

We laughed with relief and shook his hand as we introduced ourselves. He led us through rows of cars to where he'd parked. A well-proportioned lady, elegantly dressed, stepped out of the car.

"*Akwaba*, welcome to Ghana. I'm Janet, Afua's niece."

"Hello, hello, nice to meet you," Peabody said. She has a booming voice, but when she's excited it booms even more. She turned to Marie and me. "This is my cousin Yvonne," I shook Janet's hand. "And this is my daughter Marie." Marie grinned broadly as always and shook Janet's hand.

"Where's Afua?" Peabody asked as she scanned the crowd in the parking area. "Sorry I couldn't contact her about our flight delay but I guessed she would've checked with the airport and heard we were delayed for two days."

"That's okay, we did. She sends her apologies for not meeting you, but don't worry, I'll take care of you all." As if it were an afterthought, Janet added, "Her brother passed away last night."

"Oh no!" Peabody said. "I'm so sorry." She placed one hand on her forehead and for a moment I expected her to burst into tears. "What a time to visit poor Afua."

I thought it was rather ironical that Afua had been inviting Peabody to visit Ghana for the past 35 years but she never did. Finally she makes the journey, the flight is delayed for 48 hours, and Afua's brother dies the night before she arrives! I recalled my grandmother's wise words when things didn't work out as planned, "Everything happens for a reason." We were sorry for Afua's loss but if anything good could come out of a death, it did expose us to an interesting aspect of Ashanti culture that we wouldn't have experienced otherwise.

Janet was a charming attractive woman and keen to take care of her aunt's guests. Two cars were in the airport parking lot ready to transport us along with our six large pieces of luggage. We piled into one car with Janet while George drove the other car, an SUV, with most of our baggage. I realized then, that Afua alone wouldn't have been able to take us all.

The cars swung out of the airport grounds and onto a major road.

"You'll be staying at Koby's Hotel," Janet said. "It's a little way out of the city of Accra. Aunt Afua's nephew Ken, is my older brother; he owns it. You'll be comfortable and safe there. Tomorrow you will go to Kumasi."

"Thank you very much, Janet," Peabody said. "It's really kind of you to take the time to do this."

"Will you be going with us to Kumasi?" I asked. She seemed like a working woman, but I thought I would ask anyway.

"No, but George will accompany you. You'll need two cars for all of you and your luggage anyway. I'll go to Kumasi on Wednesday to pay my respects."

Because her uncle had died on Sunday, I assumed Wednesday would be closer to the funeral.

Koby's Hotel was off the beaten track. We drove for about thirty minutes on main roads then turned onto a narrow lane. It was dark, without streetlights and unpaved. The driver swerved, meandered and drove slowly, using his high beam as he tried to avoid numerous potholes.

Why would anyone travel this distance on such a deplorable road to use the hotel?

Finally, we arrived at the end of the lane and our car stopped in front of a tall metal gate. The driver tooted his horn and a man peeked through an opening. He recognized Janet, who was sitting in the front, and opened the gate. The driver drove in and parked at the side of the building; George pulled up beside him. Both men removed our luggage and Janet led us inside the hotel to a small lobby. The driver placed the last suitcase inside.

"How much is the fare?" I asked.

George didn't give him a chance to reply.

"You don't pay anything," he said with a thick accent. "Aunt Afua gave instructions that she will take care of all of your expenses, taxi, hotel, and food. Please don't worry yourself."

Peabody and I exchanged glances. What could we do but thank him? We didn't know the culture and while we were prepared to pay our expenses, we certainly didn't want to offend anyone, least of all our host.

"We'll find a way to make up for it," I whispered to Peabody. She nodded in agreement.

The main building of Koby's Hotel was a neat, two-storey structure painted white with a red-brownish terra cotta roof. Immediately behind, forming a part of the complex, was a one-storey building that contained six apartments. The receptionist was friendly and greeted us warmly. She led us to the second floor. We entered a large spacious room with two double beds and an ensuite bathroom. A colour TV stood on a commode in front of the beds. A small balcony at the front overlooked the street. Janet and the receptionist stood in the centre of the room as we inspected it. After observing satisfied looks on our faces the receptionist turned to Peabody.

"Everything fine, Ma'am?"

"Perfect. We'll be okay here."

"Did you want anything for the night?" Janet asked.

"How about some tea?" I asked.

"No problem, maybe some bread, too?"

"Yes, bread, too, please," Marie said with glee. She was our family's great bread lover.

It was about 11 p.m.; Janet had to leave.

"Well ladies, nice to meet you all," she said. "Have a good night. I have to go back to Accra. My brother and the girls here will take good care of you."

"Thanks again, Janet," I said. "We'll see you in Kumasi, right?"

"Yes, see you there Wednesday. Goodnight." She left the room with the receptionist.

I slipped into the bathroom. It was spotless, but there were only two bath towels on the rack.

"Please bring us another bath towel and another pillow when you're coming up," I called out to the receptionist as she descended the stairs.

"All right, I will."

After we had our bread and tea we couldn't wait to take refreshing showers. Although there was hot and cold water, with temperatures in the 30s, a cool shower was all we needed. We slipped into our beds and in no time we were out like an uncovered candle in a storm.

A chorus of cock-a-doodle-dos awoke me the next morning. The hotel was located on an obscure street, but it seemed there were houses nearby. With eyes still filled with sleep, I checked my watch on the nightstand. I'd switched it to Ghana time the moment we arrived at the airport. It was 6 o'clock. I rolled out of bed and pulled the drapes slightly back and peeked outside. I had a good view of the road we'd travelled during the night. Gaping potholes were clearly visible. The earth was parched and red in patches.

By 7:30 Peabody and Marie had washed, dressed and joined me in the small dining room just beyond the lobby downstairs. From two windows at the side we looked out at the small parking area and the landscape beyond. A pleasant girl dressed in a white blouse and navy blue skirt came to take our orders.

"Good morning. What would you ladies like dis morning?"

Several items were listed on the menu. Eggs and ham we knew; others we didn't.

"What's good here?" I asked.

"De Cassava fish is good."

"Cassava fish? I've never heard of it. What's it like?"

"Kinda like grouper, Miss."

We all decided to try it, but also ordered eggs and bread and butter. While we waited for our order, I glimpsed movement at one of the windowsills. Vivid memories of my first trip to Ghana and Nigeria came rushing back. Movements meant a creature was at hand! I kept my eyes glued to the window. An ash-gray lizard crawled into view.

"Oh no!"

"What? What?" Marie asked. Her eyes enlarged through her glasses like a bug-eyed fish, and her face became deadly serious.

"A lizard."

"Where? Where?" She sprang from her chair with alacrity. I've known Marie since birth and in all those years I'd never seen her so nimble. For one moment I thought she was going to jump on top of the table.

"On the windowsill," I said, keeping my eyes focused on the reptile.

Just then the waitress returned carrying a tray with a teapot, sugar and milk.

"There's a lizard over there," I said, pointing to the window. "We won't be able to eat our breakfast until we know it's gone."

She looked at Marie and me as if we were lunatics, then I saw the dawning on her face. She gave us a toothy smile.

"You're afraid of lizards?"

"You got that right. Get it out of here!"

She walked over to the window and flapped the tea towel she'd held in her hand, and shooed the lizard away. Only then did we settle down to eat our breakfast.

Two hours later we were on our way to Kumasi. George chauffeured us in his SUV while another man drove a Toyota with our luggage. The adventure was about to begin.

FIVE

ROAD TO KUMASI

Once you have set foot on the huge continent called Africa, you never seem to get enough of it. Small wonder then that so many European men and women have visited and never left. Small wonder that so many European countries: Belgium, France, Portugal, and Britain (the largest culprit) have carved out their chunk of it. All the modern luxuries of the west may not be available everywhere, but it is the spirit of the place that holds you captive. Eddy Harris, author of *Native Stranger*, aptly described it as "an abyss of mystery." You want to explore it, learn about it, experience it and become totally absorbed in its beauty and mystique, despite the bad rap the media has given it. Africa must be one of the closet places to God; at least that is how I feel when I'm there. It has a beauty and serenity that leaves you in awe.

I'd travelled the road to Kumasi from Accra on my first visit to Ghana, but it was a new adventure for my cousins. I was excited to experience it all over again with them. I was also curious to see what changes, good or bad, had occurred in five years.

The SUV ate up the miles and George, being the quiet type, said very little. Ghana is divided into 10 administrative regions, each with its own capital. After leaving the Greater Accra region, we drove through several towns in the Eastern Region and through Koforidua, its capital. From the road we saw women making clothes in small shops. We heard the whirr of old sewing machines with foot pedals going full blast.

All along the road, I observed churches of every possible denomination. Amazed by this, I retrieved a notepad from my purse, and began to jot down the names: The Apostolic Church of Ghana, The Church of Christ, Presbyterian, Methodist, Jehovah's Witness, Catholic. They were all there and this was only on one road. The Europeans had done a great job of bringing their religion to the natives. Later I had reasons to question whether it was so great after all. My misgiving was not so much about bringing Christianity to the region, for I have a strong religious faith; it concerned the way the missionaries had taught the natives and the ramifications it had caused based on its application.

At noon we saw many students walking along the road. They were dressed neatly in uniforms; the boys wore peach or brown shirts with brown pants while the girls sported peach blouses and brown tunics.

"They're so cute," Marie said. She wasn't one for saying much but was a keen observer who sopped up details like *Bounty*.

"We wore uniforms when we went to school, too," Peabody said.

"It's a British thing," I said. "Every country that they colonized, the children wear uniforms. It's a good thing, though, no competition with the haves and have-nots. Kids don't need to steal their classmate's clothes; there's no distraction; it's all the same. I remember my elementary school uniform was a navy blue tunic with a white blouse."

"I wore the same thing and I was many years before you," Peabody said.

In Eastern Region the roads consisted of two lanes in fairly good condition. The grass along the sides of the road was thick and tall, the vegetation, green and lush. Cassava plants sprouted up everywhere; some so tall they were used as hedges. We passed fields of corn and banana trees, with palm trees and coconut trees mingled together. Tall majestic trees with silver trunks grew in abundance in the towns and villages. I was curious about these trees. As we drove by a cluster of them, I touched George on his arm.

"George, what is the name of those tall trees over there?"

"Those are cedar trees. They make plywood from them."

I kept a keen eye out for different types of cars and was amazed by the changes in five years. On my first visit, every second car was a Peugeot and most of them were battered and decrepit. Now most of the cars were Toyotas, Opels and Subarus, most in good condition. It seemed the Japanese had knocked out the French and captured the auto market.

Peabody stared out the window, awestruck by the place. "Look, look Yvonne, the dirt is red just like in Manchester."

We'd grown up in Manchester, a parish in the south central part of Jamaica, where the dirt was red and rich in bauxite. It had been a challenge to keep white clothes white there, but we did.

"Yes, brings back memories of Jamaica, eh?" I said.

"You got that right. Not only the soil but the vegetation."

"I wonder if they've tested the soil here for bauxite."

"Probably not," Peabody said. "You know how things are slow in these parts." She'd arrived with much skepticism about Africa and I hoped she would overcome it during our visit.

George overheard the conversation and defended his country. "We have bauxite. They mine it in Western Region, Ashanti Region and Eastern Region. Ghana is the third largest producer in Africa."

"Okay, I'm glad to hear it," Peabody said.

We began to play a game of tree recognition, shouting out the names of the plants we knew from the Caribbean as we spotted them.

"Almond!" I said. "Look at how green and glossy the leaves are."

Peabody became like a kid opening presents on Christmas morning.

"Breadfruit tree." She pointed to a tree laden with large green fruits.

"We call it Bebo in Ghana," George said.

"I suppose when it came to the Caribbean they Englisized it and called it breadfruit," I said. We all laughed and I imagined the tree-naming ceremony.

"Look, avocado trees, cocoa trees, mango trees," Peabody said. "But this place is big Jamaica."

"Can you believe it?" I asked, caught up in the nostalgia of our ancestral home.

A gentle mountain range, not very high, loomed in the distance. In the foreground I spotted a familiar plant covered in clusters of beautiful cup-shaped orange flowers. As children in Jamaica we used to pick the buds of this plant before they opened into flowers; then we'd squeeze their soft pointed ends. Warm liquid would spurt from them. For the life of me I couldn't remember the name.

"Hey Peabody, do you know that plant over there with the orange flowers? What is it called again?"

"Yes I know it." She struggled to remember the name, which is unlike Peabody, the walking encyclopedia of the family. "I can't remember it now, but it will come back to me."

Marie was no help with the trivia game. Born and raised in Kingston, "under the clock" as they say, she hadn't experienced the pleasure and exposure of our rural lives. She was a city girl. She didn't know plants and wasn't interested. Most of the time she was withdrawn and absorbed in her own small world.

"How about you, George? Do you know the name?"

"Sorry, no."

We saw many more of these trees all across Ghana as we travelled throughout the country. I swore I would find out the name before we departed.

Sometime later we entered a small town called Jumaqu.

"I just love the names of these places," Peabody said.

"Sounds romantic, don't they?" I said.

At Oseum, we stopped to buy fresh coconuts in the husk being sold along the side of the road. We drank sweet, cool water straight from the large fruits. After we'd quenched our thirst we asked the vendor to cut them open so we could eat the thick white jelly inside. It was a real treat for us, again a tradition in the Caribbean.

Thoughts of Adamson crept into my mind when we passed a boy holding up three dead animals tied to a stick. Adamson had told me that the name of the animal was grasscutter. The grasscutter, the size of a grown raccoon, comes from the rodent family and is a delicacy in a number of countries. He'd said, "It is the sweetest meat," as he smacked his lips. The animals held by the boy, seemed to be partially cooked, barbecued to some degree. I couldn't imagine eating it then, or now.

We were enjoying the scenery as we chatted, laughed and reminisced when we came upon something peculiar and something I hadn't seen on my first visit. At Akodowanda, a crowd of people sauntered along the road. They were dressed in black. The women wore ankle-length dresses and had covered their heads with wraps. The men wore black traditional wrap-around garments made from metres and metres of cloth.

"What's going on out here George?" I asked.

Before he could reply I spotted the reason for the procession at the head of the crowd. A group of people carried a white coffin, holding it high as they walked. The procession followed behind, blocking traffic on the road. While we were in Ghana this became a theme; we saw many similar funeral processions along the roads in several of the small towns. I also saw coffins, some very elaborate, being sold at roadsides.

When we arrived at Belcacgek, one of many small towns, the driver of the second car indicated that he wanted to stop. He announced that he was hungry. He obviously hadn't eaten a hearty breakfast as we had. We entered a food market of sorts. The place was a ramshackle, semi-covered area with small stalls overseen by women. Cooking was taking place on open fires on the ground. The place didn't appear sanitary. I was glad that I wasn't hungry; George and my cousins weren't hungry either. We planned to wait until we reached Kumasi before we ate. The driver bought lunch – grasscutter and fufu – cost 12,000 cedis. He didn't seem to mind the filthy eating place. He gobbled down the fufu and grasscutter as if it was his last supper.

We watched a man and a woman making fufu and I swore I would never put that stuff to my lips unless I made it. Using her bare hands, the woman threw pieces of cooked cassava into a dilapidated mortar. A man pounded it with a large pestle, which had a rusty wire mesh attached to one end. The woman kept dropping in pieces of cassava and the man kept pounding. This was the beginning of the process. Near the end, the woman dipped her hands into a bucket and scooped up some water and added it to the mixture. She removed the mixture from the mortar to a bowl and kneaded it, still with her bare hands. She cut it into slabs when it was just right. Then she placed the fufu in special triangular-shaped containers. I'd seen similar odd-shaped containers for sale along the road but had no idea what they were. Now I knew. The containers were made from clay or pig iron. Large flies flitted all around, buzzing in our ears and landing wherever they liked, but the people in the stalls never seemed to notice them.

We were thirsty though, and left the driver to visit a small shop at the other end of the market. At least it seemed clean and no flies hovered there. I decided that it was time to sample the local beverage.

"Hey Marie, want to try a Ghanaian beer?"

Marie, always keen to try the suds, smiled. "Sure. Which one you're gonna get?"

"Let's start with Star beer; I remember it from last time."

George looked at us and grinned sheepishly. "You ladies drink beer?"

"Sure, why not?" I asked.

"I don't know, just surprised."

He probably thought we were a bunch of Prima Donnas. I ordered three beers at 5,000 cedis each. Peabody doesn't drink; she ordered bottled water.

Standing at the counter of the little shop, I raised my bottle.

"Let's not forget this day, Marie. Here at the roadside bar at Belcacgek, you had your first Star beer, in fact, your first Ghanaian beer. Cheers." We banged our bottles together and clinked them against George's bottle too.

"I'll put it in my journal," Marie said.

She withdrew a hardcover book from her large purse and scribbled a few sentences. As the days went by, I think she recorded everything about the trip she could possibly cram into her journal. I suspect she'd been watching a lot of Oprah.

Soon we were on our way again. The car needed gasoline and we came upon a Shell gas station two kilometres later. The other gas companies I saw in Ghana were Mobile and Total. Luck was on our side because as we arrived at the outskirts of the city of Kumasi, George announced that the car had a flat tire. He was able to drive slowly to a tire shop on the main drag.

The mechanic repaired the tire in no time and we continued on the last leg of our journey. We pulled up in the parking lot of a large hotel, which was several stories high. Arrangements had been made for Ilene, Afua's daughter, to meet us there. She arrived within 10 minutes, dressed in black. We followed her Toyota in convoy to her home.

A pleasant surprise awaited us. Ilene lived in the most gorgeous house; it could have easily been in Hollywood. A gateman opened a large metal gate decorated with carvings. Ilene drove in and parked in a circular driveway. Her husband's Mercedes Benz was parked in the yard under the shade of a large frangipani tree, blanketed with delicate white flowers. George and the other driver parked behind Ilene's car. To the right, along the side of the fence, a lively garden displayed a spectrum of flowers. Red, orange and fuchsia bougainvilleas, pink and yellow hibiscus, and dahlias of various colours bloomed in profusion. We entered the house through an exquisite foyer with gleaming hardwood floors. From there, we stepped down into a huge sunken living room containing a magnificent Persian rug and sank into comfortable sofas. A big-screen TV played a movie in progress. The dining room was off to the left. The table, that seated 12 comfortably, was already set, waiting for us. A handsome man of medium build entered from a room beyond the dining room. He had the ease and appearance of someone long used to civilized comforts.

Ilene introduced us. "This is David, my husband."

"So nice to meet you, David," Peabody said.

We all shook David's hand.

"*Akwaba*, welcome," he said.

"Your home is lovely, David," I said, looking around.

"Thank you. Let me show you outside."

He steered us to a patio door and we strolled out onto an exquisitely landscaped backyard. We gazed at a swimming pool decorated with blue and white tiles around the circumference. The water, azure from reflecting the sky, looked inviting. The courtyard was paved, and beyond it, the lawn meticulously manicured. A large satellite dish stood in one corner. A tennis court was at the far end of the backyard.

Ilene did little housework; she had servants who cooked, washed, cleaned and cared for the children. As we walked back to the living room, David mentioned that they have four sons, and three lived with them.

"Our oldest is in Canada. He's studying at a college in Hamilton."

"Oh really?" I said. "That's not too far from where I live, about an hour's drive."

"Maybe I can give you his number and you can contact him."

"I would be happy to do that; at least he'll have someone not too far away that he can call if he needs anything."

"That would be kind of you. I'll give you his e-mail address before you leave."

"Speaking of e-mail, David, do you have a computer?"

"Yes I do." He looked at me as if to say, *What? Do you think we're backward here?* "Would you like to check your e-mail?"

"You read my mind, yes."

David led me through a hallway beyond the dining room to his office. He booted up the computer and in no time I was reading my hotmail and sending e-mails. It was cool to correspond with friends in Toronto from Africa.

I returned to the living room to find that one of Ilene's maids had served cold, refreshing drinks to all the guests and Peabody engrossed in conversation with David. Ilene soon announced lunch was served and we took our large appetites to the dining room. We ate a delicious meal of crab soup, fish, yams and vegetables.

After the meal, the second driver transferred our luggage to Ilene's car, bade us goodbye, and set out to return to Accra. We said goodbye to David. Peabody and I joined Ilene in her car while Marie travelled with George. We drove to our final destination.

SIX

AFUA – ASHANTI WOMAN

ILENE SWUNG her red Toyota off the main street onto a quiet residential avenue. The houses were modest and orderly with neat lawns and pretty flower gardens. She stopped in front of a large and imposing two-storey house. She stepped out and opened the white painted wrought-iron gate, drove halfway up a narrow driveway, and parked. George pulled up behind her.

"We're here," she announced.

Peabody and I exchanged glances and I read her mind as clear as a document under a magnifying glass.

Mmm, what a big helluva house. Afua must be doing well.

She'd come to Africa with the same misconception that many of us, who have never visited, have about life on the big continent. Despite the blackness of our skin, we as blacks in North America, remained trapped in the whiteness of our assimilated culture. We lost our ancestors, our history and our African culture many years ago. Our misapprehension was due to lack of information, ignorance, and unbalanced media reporting. Although she'd corresponded with Afua over the years, information was never exchanged about how well each had done. I couldn't help thinking that maybe if Afua had mentioned that she was well off and living grand, Peabody would have visited sooner.

On my previous visit to West Africa I'd learned that many of our African brothers and sisters lived very well, sometimes much better than many in North America. But like a doubting Thomas, many of us had to see it to believe. The size of the house didn't surprise me, especially after having visited Ilene's home.

As we piled out of the car, our excitement rose. Ilene led the way onto a verandah. She knocked on the large, polished wooden front door. It swung open after the second knock to reveal a tall, graceful woman, with smooth, black skin. She had dark eyes with a reddish tinge and wore large framed eyeglasses long gone out of style. She stepped out and greeted Peabody with enthusiastic hugs, kisses and laughter.

"Peabody my dear, such a long time." She spoke slowly, measuring every word.

"Afua my dear, at last I've made it to Africa," Peabody said.

"Not just Africa sister, to Kumasi and my home. *Akwaba*!" They hugged again.

Suddenly, realizing she was being impolite, Afua turned and greeted Marie and me and invited us in. She introduced us to her young niece, Nora, and her helper, a 20-year-old called Saywa. Afua had a 30-year-old daughter named Anita. She suffered from Down Syndrome and had the mind of a four-year-old child. She couldn't walk on her own. She was sitting on the floor in the living room and stared at us as if we were invaders from Mars. Saywa lived on the premises and took care of her.

Afua, the vision of an Ashanti woman, was dressed in an angle-length black dress and a black head wrap. She wore other outfits but always dressed in black during the time we spent in Kumasi. Being cognizant of her brother's death, we sobered up and extended our condolences. Ilene and George left shortly after the introductions were made.

We placed our luggage in a hallway, away from the general traffic area and sat down to exchange pleasantries and present our gifts to Afua. She discussed our living accommodations.

"This house is a duplex."

Okay, that explains the size.

"I would love for everyone to stay this side of the house but I think it will be a bit cramped." Afua's accent was slightly tainted from having lived in England, her English perfect. "Let me give you a quick tour."

The house had three bedrooms upstairs, a main bathroom and a long hallway. It also had a back porch where the maid ironed clothes and hung laundry to dry. Downstairs there was a large living room, dining room, kitchen and a powder room. The living room was cozy with two sets of sofas, several chairs and a patterned rug in the centre.

A wall-unit stood in one corner; on it several family photographs, including one of Afua's deceased husband, were displayed. A verandah stretched the full length of the building in front.

After the tour we sat on plush sofas in the living room, ready to hear more about the death of Afua's brother and all that it entailed. But Afua seemed more concerned about her guests.

"I think Marie and Yvonne might prefer to sleep on the other side of the house; it will be more comfortable. I own both sides and normally rent the other side but the tenants left a few months ago. I'm painting it and doing some minor repairs, so it's empty now but one bedroom is furnished."

"Well, let's see what it's like," I said. I wanted us to stay together, being cramped wouldn't be a big deal for me; we were a close family. Besides, we were only going to be in Kumasi for a week or so. We intended to be out and about most of the time; the house would be only for sleeping. But to please our host, Marie and I agreed to see the other side.

The duplex was attached by a low wall at the side. Each house had its individual gate and driveway. We scaled the wall easily. Afua led us to the front door. We entered and noticed that the house was identical to Afua's side. The bedroom we were to occupy was modestly furnished. I walked over to the bedroom window, drew the curtains aside and looked out. A dramatic view of the sprawling city of Kumasi stretched out before me. The bathroom across the hall was operational.

"What do you think?" Afua looked anxiously at me, then at Marie.

"It will do fine," I said.

We would have nothing to fear at nights; everyone else would be right next door.

"Okay with me, too," Marie said.

"Good. You'll spend your time over at my side when you are home, just use this for sleeping at nights."

For the next eight days, instead of walking up the driveway and using the gate, Marie and I scaled the dividing wall between the two houses each night and laughed about how we had to "Jump over the wall!" We felt like teenagers stealing out at nights. Each morning after we showered and completed our grooming, we climbed over the wall again and joined the rest of the household for breakfast.

As the days passed, it was fascinating to watch the camaraderie between Afua and Peabody. It reminded me of the times when I got together with Etaine, my best friend at high school. It was always as if time stood still. We would metamorphose into teenagers again, recollecting stories that were decades old. We would relive past moments and impersonate the people from our past. The two senior citizens did a similar thing. I learned that Afua was 70, the same age as Peabody, but they could've easily passed for 60. These women were sprightly, refusing to age. They had plump smooth skin and not a wrinkle in view. They reminisced at length about the old days in England, the bad weather, the tube, the poor living conditions and previous friends.

Peabody possessed a memory like an elephant. Of course, I knew that. She was our family's *Encyclopedia Britannica*. She had such an incredible long-term memory that she could recollect the birth date of every family member, date of death of those who had passed on, and details of every major event that took place 60 years ago.

Peabody made an excellent dinner guest, one who kept the party alive. Once she had visited me in Toronto to attend a dinner party I was hosting. During dinner she related a blow-by-blow description of the festivities that took place in Jamaica during the coronation of King George V1! Sometimes when I visited her in Rochester, she, her three daughters and I would sit around the kitchen table and share stories. Peabody usually did most of the talking. Once she recounted the story of my birth – every gory detail – as if it had occurred yesterday. Afua struggled to keep up with her friend. Some nights Peabody massaged Afua's feet. Sometimes I capitalized on the occasion and also got my feet massaged. Peabody taught Afua a new way of tying her headscarf, and Afua showed her some African ways.

It was in Kumasi that we became exposed to Ashanti tradition regarding death. At breakfast the morning after we arrived, Afua explained the situation that her brother's death had caused.

"My dear Peabody, I'm so sorry that you've arrived at such a time. I won't be able to take you and show you all around as I'd hoped because I have to mourn for my brother…."

"Oh Afua, please don't feel badly. Just to be here, to see you looking so well, is good enough for me."

We don't have to stay here long anyway; we intend to visit other parts of Ghana.

"Thanks, Sister. But you won't be stuck in the house anyway. My next-door neighbour, right behind this house, has a younger brother, Akwasi. He's not doing too much. I've arranged to lend him my car so he can take you around. I suggested some places he can take you all."

"That's so kind of you," Peabody said. "But what will you be doing all day? I know you have a business to run."

"At a time like this, no business goes on. I closed the store the moment I heard about the death. I don't think I'll open until after the funeral. I have to spend the days at the dead yard."

My curiosity was at its summit now. "So how long do you have to do this?" I asked. I assumed she would mourn until the funeral, which would probably be no later than the end of the week.

"In our tradition the family mourns for 40 days."

"What?" Peabody asked, then caught herself. She lowered her voice. ""You mourn for 40 days?"

"That's the normal period for Ashantis. But my brother converted to Christianity many years ago; he was a Methodist. He was sick for a short while and knew death was imminent so he requested that we mourn for only 21 days. The wife is carrying out his request."

Marie, who hadn't said a word since the conversation began, spoke.

"When will your brother be buried?"

"On the 21st day."

My imagination went galloping on that one. Somewhere from the crevices of my mind, and I can't imagine how this happened, a scene from my very early childhood when I was about four, came into focus. On a sheet of galvanized zinc, affixed to a wooden stand, lay a body packed with blocks of ice. If this was how they did it in Africa, in the near 38-degree temperature, that body would be rotting long before the end of 21 days. I had to ask the question.

"Where is the body being kept during this period of mourning?"

"In the morgue."

Okay, they have a morgue, no rotting body, thank God. I'm so relieved.

"Listen, I have to go now. I'll get Akwasi to take you to my brother's house tomorrow so you can give his widow your condolences."

Seeing that Afua was still dressed in black, I said, "We didn't travel with anything black, is it okay to come in our colourful summer clothes?"

"Yes, that's okay. Everyone will know you're all tourists. Just knock on Akwasi's door to let him know when you want to go out."

My cousins and I had arrived in Africa with two visas stamped in our passports, one for Ghana and one for Mali. We needed to make arrangements for Mali. I felt that we should do so as soon as possible. It was a good time to ask Afua how we should go about it.

"Afua, before you go, can you advise us on a travel agency? We plan to visit Mali but haven't arranged it yet."

"I don't know much about the arrangements from here but I'll give you a couple names. Tell Akwasi to take you to these agents in Kumasi."

"Thanks, we'll do it today," I said, taking a slip of paper with the names from her.

With that, she collected her purse, said goodbye and left. She returned at 7 p.m. to have supper with us and that was her routine for the rest of the time we spent at her home.

When I knocked on Akwasi's door at 10 o'clock he was ready to take us on a tour of Kumasi. He was a handsome 22-year-old, tall, with a good physique. He was attempting to grow a goatee and the hairs were just coming in. Later, Peabody and I soon observed that Saywa was all smiles and fluttering her lashes when he came around.

"Did you see that Saywa?" I said to Peabody on the second day. "I wonder if Afua is aware of the attraction."

"Next thing you know, baby in the back," Peabody said.

It was an inside joke between us. While travelling from Accra to Kumasi, we had noticed many young women with babies strapped to their backs. Peabody kept saying, "Baby in the back!" She now visualized Saywa in a similar position.

Afua's car was a sporty white Toyota and Akwasi seemed keen to drive it. Our first stop was at the centre of Kumasi. The town seemed larger than I remembered it on my first visit with Adamson in 1997. The last census showed the Ashanti region as the most populous in Ghana with over three and a half million people. Kumasi was a hubbub of activity. Many streets were lined with shops and stores. It bustled with vendors, shoppers and taxicabs. All taxicabs were painted on the sides with strips of blue and yellow, or black and yellow, or green and yellow, and so on.

At the main square we bought post cards as we were anxious to write to our folks and friends back in Canada and the United States to tell them we were having a good time. Kumasi's main post office was situated in the middle of the square and we mailed the cards right away. While we were writing up our cards, a group of boys, no more than eight or nine years old, swarmed us. They were selling wares and immediately assumed we were all Americans. We cracked up laughing when one boy declared, "America is second heaben! If I go to America I will never be poor!"

"That is not so," I said. "Where did you get that idea?"

"I know. I see it on TV. I hear people talking. America is second heaben."

I tried to explain the reality to him.

"You've got it wrong son; that isn't so. Everyone in America isn't rich. There are poor, homeless people there, too."

But he was adamant that it was second heaven and nothing I could say would change his mind.

"One day I will go to America. I will be rich!"

Even in Kumasi, West Africa, the misconception about the United States had an impact on innocent, naive young boys. Here was a lad, who did not refer to his country as paradise. He was born in a country with a rich heritage, rich in gold and minerals, once even called the Gold Coast and the envy of the world when Europeans – Dutch, Portuguese and English – fought to acquire it. Instead, this boy salivated over the United States, seeing it as a second heaven. Many Africans thought it was the greatest place on earth and the place where everyone was wealthy! Small wonder that so many Africans tried to get there one way or another, forsaking family, tradition, and all that they held dear. In contrast, it was heartwarming to see folks like Afua, who after living in England for many years, returned home and was undoubtedly happy to do so. She had everything she needed, lived a good lifestyle, and was comfortable. She would never leave her country again.

Akwasi took us on a whirlwind tour of Kumasi, driving up and down side streets, back streets, and all over town. People moved about like bees in a beehive, busy, bustling. He took us to one of the travel agencies on Afua's list and there we inquired about a trip to Mali. We almost fell out of our chairs when the clerk gave us the price.

"We can arrange a trip to Mali for you; Airfare will cost $700 American dollars each."

"It's $700 American dollars just for the flight?" I asked. I'd expected to pay a couple hundred dollars. "How can that be? Isn't Mali just north of Ghana?"

"Yes Madame, Burkina Faso is immediately north of us, then Mali is right after, but we don't have any direct flights there. KLM can take you but you would have to fly to Amsterdam, then fly from there to Mali."

I was flabbergasted. I then began to understand what Africa was about. This huge landmass that the western media tended to refer to as if it were a country, is a large continent containing 53 countries. These countries, although similar in many ways – inhabitants' skin colour, foods, and climate – were totally autonomous and not necessarily connected. I lived on another large continent, North America, but transportation to and from the countries occupying that landmass was fairly simple. I could fly directly from Canada to the United States or Mexico, any day of the week. I could drive to any part of the United States or take a bus or a train. Not so with Africa. Having travelled 14 hours via Amsterdam to Ghana, I most certainly wouldn't fly nearly six thousand kilometres to Amsterdam just to fly back to Africa in order to visit Mali. That was the most asinine thing I'd heard.

I discussed the matter with my cousins and we decided without hesitation that we would not spend $700 US just to be able to fly to Mali. We would forgo that trip. Akwasi stood listening to our discussion and made a suggestion.

"I tink yuh are right, I wouldn't spend so much. Why don't yuh go to Togo? You don't even have to fly dere, you can hire a driver and a car to take yuh dere."

"Is that so?" Peabody asked.

"Yes, you can get dere easy."

"But we don't have visas for Togo."

"Don't worry about dat; yuh can get it right away at de border when yuh going to cross."

"I think we should do that," I said. "I'd really hoped we would visit at least two countries while we're here."

"When will we arrange the trip?" Marie asked. She was keen to see everything.

"We should do it when we get to Tema. I'll get Pastor Ray to arrange it."

With that decision made, we began to focus on our tour of the Ashanti region.

At my request, Akwasi drove us to Barclay's Bank where I converted some travellers cheques. Then he took us home.

Later that day, a driver picked us up and took us to Ilene's house again, this time for an early supper. We sat around the elegant dining table and enjoyed a fabulous meal of soup made from crab and mushrooms, fish and fufu.

"It's strange that I was unable to swallow fufu on my first trip to Ghana, but somehow I can eat yours," I said to Ilene.

"We make it from cassava flour. Maybe the one you tried was from pounded cooked cassava. That tends to be stickier."

David made an interesting statement. "I would never eat fufu that is pounded."

"Why is that David?" I asked.

"Because it is not hygienic. In fact, I don't eat fufu outside of my home."

Having watched the woman making it at Belcacgek, I felt the same way.

Peabody was experiencing euphoria; she rolled her eyes and lapped her ears like a dog would do.

"Mmmm, this yam is delicious. I don't remember eating yam this good before."

I kicked her under the table when she took a third piece from the serving dish. "Don't get carried away; remember your diabetes," I said under my breath.

I knew she was always careful about what she ate and that she exercised regularly. She was a model diabetic, but in Ghana, exercise would be put on hold. It was therefore important that she watched her starch intake even more carefully.

With supper over, we settled into the posh sofas and David switched on the TV. Having a satellite dish provided access to many channels, but nothing interested us. I slipped away briefly to use David's computer to send more e-mails. I wanted my son, Robert, to know that we were all safe. Afterwards I returned to the living room.

"I have a video you might be interested to see," David said. His face beamed as he looked at us.

"What's it about?" I asked.

"It's the event when the Ashanti King honoured Kofi Annan in Kumasi. I take it you know who Kofi is?"

"Of course. The Secretary General of the United Nations. Every black person should know who he is."

"There was much pomp and pageantry at the ceremony. All the chiefs were there in their special Kente robes. Kofi received the highest honour at the event. Ilene and I were there; you'll see us in the film."

That explained why he was beaming. At that moment I began to understand who David was. To be invited to such an event told me that he was a part of the "establishment." How could we say no to viewing the film? He popped the video into the VCR and we sat back to watch it.

The event was something to see. I couldn't imagine another occasion where so many chiefs assembled in one place. It was a day when the higher echelon of Ashanti hierarchy put aside their egos and self-importance, and came together. They arrived in their regalia and splendour to honour a native son who had excelled. They came to say, "Well done, Kofi Annan."

At first I didn't see David and Ilene in the video, but Marie spotted them readily. "There they are!" she yelled.

David had to rewind the tape. There they were: Mr. and Mrs. Apea. I barely recognized them. They were absolutely transformed. Dressed in their traditional garb, they looked like a prince and princess. There is something regal about Ghanaian traditional clothing. When you wear them you want to hold your head high, shoulders back; you feel tall and elegant.

Kofi stood before the Ashanti King and all the chiefs and talked eloquently. He spoke with humility and pride and the huge crowd cheered until they drowned him out. Kofi Annan, Ghana's native son was an icon, a role model and a man to emulate. It was a long video but we watched it to the end. The occasion was indescribable, the costumes incredible. There was so much gold worn by the king, chiefs and attendees on their fingers, hands and other body parts that it made Fort Knox look pale. The honour shown to Kofi Annan by his countrymen was commendable. Tears welled up in my eyes as the event unfolded. It was truly a fabulous and touching affair.

We stayed at David's house until 8:30 p.m. then Ilene drove us back to base camp.

SEVEN

ASHANTI DEATH

A DEATH IN the family is an unhappy time in everyone's life. It matters not whether you are black or white, Anglo or African. Growing up in rural Jamaica had exposed me to certain traditions regarding death that are still practiced today, but to a lesser degree. The rituals performed were never explained but I have no doubt that various aspects were brought to the island by our African ancestors.

I'll always remember when my grandfather died. One hot August day I was absorbed in a discussion in my history class about William of Orange when the news arrived on campus. The headmaster called me to his office and sent me home. I lived six miles from high school and while buses were readily available in the morning and evening rush hours, they were few during the day. I arrived home several hours later. Grandfather's body had been washed, dressed and placed on his bed.

Agatha, a village matriarch, came to visit grandmother. I'd rarely seen grandma's bedroom door closed during the day, but she had closed it after Agatha arrived.

What were they doing in there?

Being 13 and curious, I listened at the door and peeked through the keyhole. I couldn't believe my eyes. Agatha removed a pair of scissors from her bag and snipped a wad of grandma's pubic hair and handed it to her. Grandma placed the wad of hair in her dead husband's hand. She glared at the corpse lying on the bed.

"Take it, take it, and don't come back here!" she ordered.

Agatha then removed a pair of red baggy underwear from her bag and commanded grandma to put them on. I'd seen enough; I rushed from the door.

A wake was another tradition practiced in the village. It was held for three consecutive nights following a death. At this event, neighbours, family members, friends and even strangers, came at dusk to the house of the deceased. The aroma of coffee permeated the air as large pots of the brew were made. Bottles of white and amber rum appeared on the dining table as well as many loaves of hard-dough breads, sliced and buttered. Sometimes, depending on the financial status of the grieving family, fried sprats were added.

There was always a lead singer among the night-watchers. This person, usually male, led the audience in singing hymns. The tunes were never sung as lively as they were done in church. Each line was drawn out, leaving a sombre spectre in the air. The leader shouted out the words of the first line then sang it with the audience joining in, then did the same for each line of all the hymns. Between the drawn-out melancholy singing of hymns, drinking of black coffee and rum, and eating of hard-dough bread, the mourners passed the hours until near midnight when they slowly dispersed. The deceased was usually buried within three days. There would be one final gathering to sing, eat and drink – on the ninth night after death, aptly called the "Ninenight." This was the extent of mourning for the dead as I knew it during my childhood.

I was overly curious to see and hear more about death traditions in Ashanti culture, to discover if there were any connections with my Jamaican experience. I was already floored by the information that the mourning period lasted 40 days and that close family members would literally abandon their businesses for such an extended period of time.

Two days after we arrived in Kumasi, Akwasi drove us to the dead man's home. I won't soon forget the experience. We arrived at an imposing gate. It was opened and Akwasi drove up the long driveway. I soon realized that the property was sizable and that the owner was wealthy. A large house stood sheltered by several mature trees. I crouched in the back seat of the car and removed my movie camera from its pouch and began to film discreetly. I didn't want anyone to see me doing so as I wasn't sure if it was appropriate. A white tent erected on the lawn in front of the house was unoccupied. Hundreds of red resin chairs were stacked under a tree, ready to be used. A sound system placed just beyond the tent played haunting African music. It was not intrusive, as the volume was turned down to provide background music.

Akwasi parked the car on the grass among several other cars and we walked toward the house. About fifty men and women sat in red resin chairs on a large, elevated veranda. They were all dressed in different variations of black – some with patterns, and some without. Everyone wore thick black sandals, and the women had black scarves on their heads.

Afua greeted us at the steps leading to the verandah and introduced us to the widow who was sitting among the crowd. We expressed our condolences and she acknowledged by nodding her head. Despite puffy eyes, she was attractive with a light complexion. One of the men promptly placed more chairs among the crowd for us to sit. My cousins and I sat with the crowd for an hour. There was nothing to say or do, we simply sat and observed. At intervals, the widow burst into tears. Some of the ladies got up to console her and they cried, too. As if on queue, some of the mourners stood up at intervals and walked among the crowd. They reminded me of a receiving line. With heads held down, they never made eye contact; they just shook hands and sat down again. While I sat there observing the ritual, tears smarted my eyes; it was such a sombre affair.

Being a widow in this culture must be tougher than any other. Imagine going through this procedure for 40 days!

After Afua returned home that night, we had supper together then retired to the living room. Several relatives arrived at the house and I noticed they were dressed in black outfits made from the same material as Afua's dresses. I couldn't imagine that it was the only black cloth available in the town.

"Afua, how come your relatives all wear dresses made from the same material as yours?" I asked after the visitors departed. "Is it planned?"

She laughed. "You're very observant, Yvonne. Let me tell you a bit about how funerals are done here."

My ears pricked up. I retrieved a notebook from by purse and moved closer to her on the sofa.

"First of all, before one week after a death, the head of the family calls a meeting of all immediate family members. We call this person the *Absuapanyin*. It's usually a male family member. At the meeting they decide on all funeral arrangements, how much to spend, how much each member will contribute, which day to bury, etcetera, etcetera. Sometimes they decide to "cut a cloth," meaning they select bolts of the material to make the mourning clothes. That was done for us, which is why we wear the same material."

"Do they wear the same style?" Marie asked.

"No, not necessarily; people select their own styles. By the way, if the deceased is a child or young person, we usually wear black and white."

My appetite for information was not fully appeased, but I decided to withhold further questions on the subject for now to give Peabody and her friend time to continue reminiscing.

Just before noon on Sunday we returned with Afua to the grieving widow's home. Afua mentioned that there wouldn't be any visitors at that time. She steered us into the living room. The room was grandiose and tastefully decorated with a high ceiling and sparkling chandeliers. A large Persian rug with black background and beige and brown patterns, so thick that my feet sank into it, covered the centre of the floor. Arranged around the room were two sets of sofas and several exquisite chairs. A pair of chairs with gold trim caught my attention. An old woman sat in one. An Ashanti-style stool, upholstered in white leather, stood conspicuously beside an intricate mahogany coffee table. The number 80 was embossed in studs on the stool's centre. Afua explained that it was a gift to the deceased for his 80th birthday. A bookshelf stacked with books and many photographs of family members stood at one end of the room.

The widow, dressed in black, sat on one of the sofas. She had seven adult children; between them, they had produced 22 grandchildren. Two of her daughters hovered about in a smaller sitting room toward the back of the main living room.

Afua introduced us to the woman sitting in the golden chair.

"This is Nana Takyiaw."

"I'm Queen Mother for Amoamain Village not far from here," she said. She was a buxom woman, dressed in the traditional black mourning dress with the head wrap.

After we conveyed our condolences again, Peabody became engrossed in a conversation with Nana. I went to sit beside the widow. I wanted to be respectful, but curiosity and a burning desire to learn about the culture couldn't be harnessed.

I spoke softly to her. "Mrs. Ntiem, I'm interested to hear about a few things. I hope you don't mind if I ask you some questions."

"No I don't mind; go ahead." She smiled.

"Tell me about some of the traditions that an Ashanti woman has to observe when her husband dies?"

She thought about the question for a while. "Well, I can't eat any food that comes out of the ground."

"Are you serious? Food like yams?"

"Yes, no yams, bread, rice, nothing like that."

"Wow." There wasn't much more I could say as I thought about it. Didn't almost everything we consume come out of the ground? I suppose fruits that are borne above the ground would be an exception. Maybe she could eat breadfruits and bananas.

Mrs. Ntiem continued without my prompting.

"I have to be bathed by someone everyday from the day my husband died until he's buried."

"My goodness." I blushed purple then recovered. "I guess you have to forget about your pride, eh?" I said nonchalantly as I pictured the widow in her sorrow being prodded and scrubbed by a stranger. It was difficult to visualize it for myself.

"Yes, I don't think about it. I also wear special beads around my waist."

I stared at her body, searching with my eyes to glimpse the beads, but they were concealed under her loose-fitting dress and not noticeable.

"I'm supposed to mourn for 40 days, but my husband requested we mourn for only 21 days, so I'm doing that. I must put my husband's sandals in front of the bedroom door. I'm not going to bother with that though." She hissed her teeth in defiance. She was younger than Afua which meant she was more than twenty years younger than her husband. I was surprised to hear her say this, but it was obvious that she was liberal and would only adhere to some of the traditions. Not wanting to appear brash, I thanked her for sharing.

I turned to Nana. "It's really nice to meet you. I've never met a Queen Mother before."

"This lady was married to my brother who died eight years ago," Afua said.

Nana Takyiaw stared at me with interest, then demonstrated that she wasn't bashful. "Are yuh married?" she asked.

Taken aback by the question, I answered before I could think. "No, I'm not."

"A nice lady like yuh? I can find a husband fah yuh."

"No, no! No husband," I said. I couldn't begin to imagine what she would have sourced for me.

What on earth made her think that I wanted a husband? And if I did, why would I seek one in Ghana?

She seemed disappointed. I was sorry about it, but I couldn't allow a husband-hunt.

An hour later a group of men wearing white robes arrived. Because Afua had said that the widow would not have visitors that day, I asked who they were.

"Oh, they're from the men's fellowship group at the church of my brother."

The deceased had converted to Christianity many years earlier. Afua had explained that he had seven wives previously, and from those unions he fathered 45 children. But after conversion, he kept only one wife, the now grieving widow. Although curious to know what became of the other wives and their children, I refrained from asking. It was these kinds of issues that made me wonder if Christianity had helped to make Africans better or worse off.

The men in white robes never entered the house. They stayed on the verandah where they sang a few hymns, said a prayer, then marched quietly away in single file.

EIGHT

SIGHTS AND SOUNDS OF GHANA

I WAS BOISTEROUSLY awakened at 4 a.m. for the third consecutive morning by a loud noise, and the sound of a horn blaring in the distance. An hour later, just as I'd settled back into a contented sleep, the blaring started again, followed by chanting. Later, I learned that it was the muezzin at the Muslim Mosque in the city announcing the call to prayer and a new day. I realized that I had better get used to the noise; it was a daily occurrence. Besides the muezzin, adding to the mayhem, roosters began to crow and birds to chirp about the same time. Strange, I heard no dogs barking. The city was coming to life.

On this day, Akwasi planned to take us on a tour of landmarks in the Ashanti region. My cousins and I joined Afua at the dining table and Saywa served us a big breakfast of yams, fried eggs, bread and tea. As usual, Afua departed after breakfast for her daily trip to her deceased brother's home. I walked with her to the gate and on the way back, I knocked on Akwasi's door. I was raring to go on another adventure. He was ready. With cameras loaded and bottled water stashed in our totes, Peabody, Marie and I piled into the Toyota and we set out.

"So where are we going today?" I asked Akwasi as the car merged onto the main street.

"Is a surprise. Yuh'll see when we get dere." He turned his handsome head and grinned at me sitting beside him.

"Okay, if that's how you want to play it," I said. We laughed and decided to go along with it. He was a pleasant young man and keen to please the visitors.

"Let's just sit back and enjoy the scenery," Marie said from the back seat.

So we sat back and gazed at the landscape and exchanged thoughts about the things we saw as the car meandered along the circuitous roads.

The Ashanti Region, home of the Ashanti people, and one of Ghana's major ethnic groups, is a large area nestled in the south central part of the country. Afua had assured us that the region offered many sights for us to see. On a previous journey, I'd visited Kumasi and spent a day and a night, and although Adamson had packed in as much sightseeing as he could, I'd only seen a few places. With several days and a driver and car at our disposal, we were excited to view the land and Akwasi was enthusiastic to take us on a whirlwind tour of his part of the country.

We ascended lofty hills and descended through delicious green valleys. In one place we were engulfed by a plantation of hectares and hectares of low verdant trees that seemed uniformly planted. The leaves grew in clusters, were glossy and elongated with conspicuous main veins. Some of the taller trees bore small green fruits in bunches like grapes.

"Yuh see dose trees over dere?" Akwasi asked.

We nodded.

"Dats de Karite tree. Dey make Shea butter from de nuts in de fruits. I heard dat one of the politicians own dat land."

So that's the plant from whence it came.

In Toronto, I'd recently bought a clump of Shea butter at a trade show, after the sales person had persuaded me that it was excellent for washing the face, and that it had the constituent to make skin plump and smooth.

Just up ahead we came upon some students dressed in uniforms; they carried bundles of firewood on their heads.

"Must be a tough life for those kids," Peabody said, sympathy heavy in her voice.

I thought, how quickly we forget. Growing up in rural Jamaica, while we never had to hunt and carry firewood in the mornings before school, we had to haul buckets of water from our tank to fill containers in the kitchen, water that would be used for cooking and washing dishes each day. I thought that was a tough life.

"They're used to it," Akwasi said.

The motor whined as the car laboured up another steep hill. It felt as if we were at a peak and I prayed that the car did not roll backwards. With eyes glued to the landscape, I noticed that we were surrounded by rugged mountains, one peak culminating into another. The vegetation was incredibly lush. Banana plants with their wide succulent leaves, coconut, cocoa, and almond trees were green and fresh, all unfazed by the intense heat of the sun. The sky was cobalt blue, dotted with cotton-candy clouds; it was a landscape artist's dream. Sitting in the front of the car, as I'd done on most of our trips with Akwasi, I always kept on eye on both speedometer and odometer and jotted down distance occasionally. We had travelled just over 27 kilometres of extremely winding roads. The sun rode high in the sky; it penetrated the atmosphere and seeped into our skins like body lotion.

I heard the distinct sound of a change in the engine and realized that we were descending.

"Look over to your right," Akwasi said.

We did and were taken by surprise. Through a clump of trees, rays of the sun were hitting a large area that sparkled and shimmered. Heat vapours rose from it. The view was so spectacular; it took our breath away.

"What is it?" Peabody asked.

"It's a lake." Akwasi laughed as he watched the surprise on our faces. It was the effect he'd anticipated.

"A lake in the middle of the Ashanti region?" I asked.

"Yes. When we get down dere yuh'll get some information about it."

I'm accustomed to lakes in Canada; they're natural phenomena based on the ice age and glacial action, but I'd never thought of lakes in Africa except Lake Victoria and Lake Tanganyika.

"I never knew Ghana had a lake except the Volta which I know is man-made. Is it the Volta?" Excitement poured into my veins. After all, the Volta was famous, a man-made wonder.

"No, it's Lake Bosumtwi."

"Lake what?"

"Bos-um-twi," Akwasi said slowly, emphasizing each syllable

We descended the mountain much faster than we had ascended the other side. At the foot of the mountain before Akwasi parked the car, a group of young men swarmed us. Akwasi yelled at them to back off.

A middle-aged man walked over to us as we exited the car. He was dressed shabbily. He took charge, asserting himself as an unofficial guide.

"Ladies, welcome to Lake Bosumtwi." He turned to the group of boys who had pushed forward again. "Step back, people."

"Thank you," we said in unison.

"You wanted to have a look at the lake?" the man asked.

"Sure, are you in charge?" I asked.

Looking around, I observed a large building erected a short distance from the lake. From its construction, like the shops in town, you could tell it was once a guest house and entertainment centre; now it languished in ruins.

"There isn't anyone in charge as such but I can tell you some things about the lake." His accent was heavy but his English was good.

I guess he expects a fee.

He walked with us to the edge of the lake, determined to act the part of a guide. A large expanse of water was spread out before us. Many houses were scattered on the hillside, skirting the lake on the opposite side. A battered old jeep arrived and four boys and a white man promptly jumped from it and dived into the lake.

Great day for it; I wouldn't mind doing the same.

By now the sun had reached its zenith. It was hot to the point of suffocating. We sweated profusely.

Peabody became snarky and turned to the self-appointed guide.

"Okay Mister, what do you know about this lake?"

That was the cue he'd been waiting for. He rattled off some interesting information that I quickly jotted down.

"This is the largest natural lake in Ghana. It is 16 kilometres wide, 20 kilometres long and 78 metres deep. The total area is 72 kilometres or 19 square miles."

I was awestruck; it just didn't seem natural. Totally encircled by mountains, it was as if the lake had been planted there. But the *guide* said it was natural, not man-made.

"This is so fascinating," I said. "How did such a lake come to be in the middle of the region?"

"We have many stories about how it was formed. One story, the one most people believe, says it was created by the impact of a meteor."

That made sense because it was surrounded by steep hills. It could have been a crater.

"It is very sacred to the Ashanti people," he said.

"Oh really? I guess there are legends about it I suppose?"

"Yes. Some Ashantis believe that the souls of the dead come here to say farewell to the God Twi."

Marie looked around sharply. She was probably looking to see souls!

To our right, three boys chattered and laughed. They seemed to be having a good time as they threw out their fishing rods and reeled them in.

"What are they catching?" Marie asked.

"They catch a lot of tilapia in this lake, but there're about 10 other types of fish in it too."

This sent me pondering. If the lake was formed from the impact of a meteor, where did the water and fish come from?

"Are there rivers flowing into the lake?" I asked.

"No, only some streams. It gets mainly rainwater."

"And what about the houses all around?"

"There are 28 different villages over there." He spread his arms indicating the width of the lake.

We would have stayed longer, but the heat was unbearable. We thanked the *guide*, gave him a few cedis, then piled into the car. Akwasi drove back up the hill.

"Do we have the pleasure of knowing where we are going this time?" Peabody asked as we levelled off.

"Okay, no more surprises. We're going to Obuasi."

"And what is there?" I asked.

"You know that Ghana has gold, right?"

"Yes, that we know."

In my research I had learned that gold had been mined in Ghana for centuries. The country was once called the Gold Coast. Ghana achieved Independence from Britain on March 6, 1957, a momentous occasion, as it was one of the first sub-Saharan African colonies to gain its independence. With Kwame Nkrumah as leader, it discarded the colonial name of the Gold Coast.

"Obuasi is one of de gold towns. It have a gold mine and I hope we will get dere in time to visit it."

"Sounds good to me," I said.

All my life I'd never been into any mines, gold or otherwise. I was excited about the prospect of visiting one. I visualized us dressed in overalls and hard hats with little lights on top just like I'd seen in the movies. It would make for a good photo opportunity.

As we came closer to Obuasi, I noticed an area near the road. It was swampy with murky water. Many shrubs filled with hundreds of birds' nests jutted out of the swamp. Tiny bright yellow birds chirped loudly as they flew in and out of the nests. It was like an aviary there.

"Those birds are beautiful," I said. "What are they, Akwasi?"

"Dey are called weaver birds."

Marie asked him to stop. She and I got out of the car and took pictures of some of the clumps of nests and the exotic birds.

At the town of Bekwai a crowd of students dressed in uniforms were walking on the road. We assumed the school day had ended. Hundreds of broken down, ramshackle houses lined the street. Palm trees and coconut trees swayed as a slight breeze ticked their leaves.

Finally, at 5 p.m. we arrived in Obuasi, a large bustling town. The town screamed of poverty, disease and death. The area was in terrible condition. The most deplorable, dilapidated shacks I'd seen so far lined the street. A schoolhouse stood in disrepair. Vendors sold goods from stalls set up along the way. Goats trotted across the bumpy road as if they were in charge. Fences, made from galvanized zinc, were rusted and falling down by the roadside. The whole scene was brown and depressing.

I thought of the village where I grew up near Mandeville, Jamaica. Bauxite was mined there. Alcan was the first mining company to start extracting the ore, but other companies like Kaiser and Reynolds followed. It took only a few years of mining operation there for a remarkable transformation to occur. The area prospered and the best roads and some of the most gorgeous houses were built. It is now the home of many returning residents – Jamaicans who had emigrated to England, the United States and Canada in the 1960s. It is a place where you would love to live. Why had a similar thing not occurred here in Obuasi?

"Did you say this is a gold mining town?" I asked Akwasi, totally astounded by its appearance.

"Yes, dey say it is the richest gold mining town in de world."

I looked at the place, the people, the condition of the roads and was appalled; so were my cousins.

"It's obvious that the wealth from all that gold has not filtered down to the residents," Peabody said.

"Yuh're right," Akwasi said. "It's so bad, dey had a showdown here a couple years ago about dat, but tings are still bad."

We arrived at the main gate of the mine. A guard at the small gatehouse opened a tiny window.

"Can I help you folks?"

"I have some tourists here and we want to tour de mine."

"Sorry folks, you're too late." the guard said. "The last tour was 4 p.m."

We were disappointed.

"That's too bad," Marie said. "What do we do now?"

"I'll just drive around de town a little," Akwasi said.

He drove around the town for a short time, but the place seemed too depressing. Soon we headed back toward Kumasi.

Another day Akwasi took us to the Manhyia Palace. Once the home of Ashanti kings, it is now a museum. A new palace was constructed nearby. I'd visited the Manhyia Palace on my first trip to Ghana and remembered it vividly. At that time the reigning Asantehene was Otumfuo Opoku Ware 11. That king died in 1999 at age 80, after ruling his people for 29 years. A new Asantehene, Otumfuo Osei Tuti, now ruled the kingdom, *The Golden Stool*. I was interested to see what changes, if any, had occurred.

We were visiting on a weekday. It was obviously a slow day; no other visitors were in sight when we purchased our tickets. The entrance fee was 5,000 cedis, a significant increase from the 2,000 cedis I'd paid five years earlier. I wasn't put out by it though. The exchange rate had been 1,700 cedis to one American dollar then; now it was 7,500 cedis to one. Inflation ran rampant.

A guide came to take us on the tour. He was about twenty-eight, medium build, with a round face and hair cut closely to the scalp. He greeted us with a smile.

"Welcome to de Ashanti Palace ladies. My name is Kofi." He observed that Marie and I had cameras hanging around our necks. "Please, yuh're not allowed to take any pickchas inside." He suddenly stared at Peabody, then grinned like a school boy. "Sorry to stare at yuh Ma'am but yu look just like my grandma."

The three of us cracked up at that. Was it a line?

"Do I really?" Peabody asked, serious as a soldier on parade. Her beautiful salt and pepper hair was evenly distributed in an unprocessed low Afro. She wore an orange, brown and beige cotton two-piece pantsuit and running shoes. With no noticeable wrinkles, one would not expect her to have a 42-year old daughter.

"Honestly, yuh are de image of her. Can I call yuh 'Grandma?' "

"Sure, Grandma is fine with me." He was a tad too old to be her grandson, but she played along.

That broke the ice. After the familiarity, we became family. Because we were the only visitors for the tour at that hour, and Peabody was adopted grandma, Kofi allowed us to keep our cameras and to take as many pictures as we liked. With my movie camera, I promptly began to film anything of interest. He led us through the palace, room after room. The wooden floor was polished and glossy. Many paintings hung on the walls but several were on the floor, leaning against walls. I gathered that work was being done to the place. One of these paintings was of the last Ashanti King and Pope John Paul 11. The palace had been rearranged and didn't seem to be as complete as it was previously. As the tour continued I noticed that many items were missing.

Kofi directed us into a room that housed effigies of former King Otumfuo Opoku Ware 11 and the Queen Mother. The workmanship was so exquisite, the statues seemed alive! Every detail from hair texture to skin colour was perfect. In another room stood an effigy of the current king. With a golden crown on head held high, he was draped in black and white batik cloth with a yellow and orange border. His right shoulder was bare with chest held out. He wore the traditional sandals and his feet rested on a low stool – he appeared regal.

"I want yuh to sit beside yuh brada and I will take yuh pickcha," Kofi said.

Obediently, the three of us sat on the edge of the statue's pedestal and Kofi took our picture.

"Did you take me looking down or up?" Peabody inquired. She was quite serious about her pose.

"Don't worry Grandma, yuh were looking up."

In another area, Kofi led us to effigies of another king and queen mother.

"This is the fust Ashanti King. His name was Prempheh 1."

"I've heard that name in Jamaica when I was growing up," I said. "I had no idea it was an Ashanti king. Our culture is certainly intertwined with these people."

We moved on and Kofi showed us an unusual sword locked in a glass display case.

"Dis sword is made out of solid gold," he said.

"There's a head on it," Marie jumped back.

"Yes, at one time, the king chopped off a man's head and dey made a replica of de head and attached it to de sword as a reminder. When de king visits de the stool house and dere is a dispute, he use de sword to settle it."

Wow, not a people to mess with.

"Look over here." Kofi directed us to an effigy of a small woman sitting in a chair. She was dressed in a maroon and white patterned skirt with a navy blue shawl draped over her shoulders. A long rifle, the type found in the 19th century, lay in her lap. "Dis is Nana Yaa Asantewaa. She is one of our greatest women heroes."

"What wonderful things did she do?" Peabody asked with a hint of sarcasm.

"Oh, is a great story; yuh should read about it some time. I will give yuh a short version: The British tried to capture de Gold Coast by exiling the Ashanti King Premph 1 in 1896. Dis didn't break the peoples' spirit so de British demanded de supreme symbol of the Ashanti people - de *Golden Stool.* On March 28, 1900, de British Governor called a meeting of all de chiefs in and around de Ashanti city, Kumasi, and ordered dem to surrender de *Golden Stool.* Dey were insulted but didn't show any outward reaction. Dey held a secret meeting and Yaa Asantewaa, who was Queen Mother of Ejisu, was dere. De chiefs were discussing how dey should make war on de white men and force dem to bring back de Asantehene. Some said dat dere should be no war; instead dey should beg the Governor to bring back King Prempeh. Yaa Asantewaa stood up and spoke. She said dat she noticed some of de chiefs were afraid to fight for de king. She said dat in de brave days of previous kings, chiefs would not sit down and see dere king taken away without firing a shot. She said no white man could have dared to speak to Ashanti chiefs in de way de Governor had spoken to de chiefs dat morning; if de Ashanti men would not fight she and de women would!

'We will fight de white men. We will fight till de last of us fall in the battlefields.'

"This speech stirred up de men and dey decided to fight de British until dey released the Asantehene. For nine months de Ashantis, led by Yaa Asantewaa, fought bravely and kept de white men in de fort. But later British reinforcements of 1,400 soldiers arrived at Kumasi. Yaa Asantewa and other leaders were captured and sent into exile to Seychelles Island."

"Isn't that an interesting story, Peabody?" I asked.

"Yes, she sounds like one of our Jamaican heroes called Nanny. She was leader of the Maroons, our runaway slaves."

I could see her mind going a hundred miles per minute. She was connecting with our history, something she'd probably never done.

"As I recall, Nanny was a small wiry woman with piercing eyes," Peabody said. "She was a young Ashanti woman, who was shipped with five brothers as slaves to Jamaica. When they arrived, island-wide slave rebellions were going on. She hated the cruelty that the female slaves suffered on the plantations. Shortly after arrival, she and her brothers escaped and joined a group of Maroons. Nanny eventually became the leader of one of the groups. She fought the British during the first Maroon war from 1720 to 1739. She practiced what they would call guerilla warfare today. They said she also had supernatural powers; she practiced obeah."

"See, Ashantis are always good warriors," Kofi said. "By de way, Nana was 60 when she fought de British. When she died in 1921 she was 81."

I thought about Peabody's brief summary of Nanny and found the parallels intriguing.

"It is so amazing that two African women, two centuries apart, separated by thousands of miles and a huge ocean, should behave in almost an identical manner," I said.

"It's amazing," Marie said. She too was intrigued. She was not one for saying much but she was an avid reader and she soaked up conversations like sponge absorbs moisture. No doubt she would put Nanny and Nana on her reading list.

We took pictures of Nana's effigy and moved on to a room with several chairs that looked regal. Three had been placed together.

"Have a seat in one of dose chairs," Kofi said, pointing to them.

We took our seats with Peabody sitting in the middle chair.

"I met my grandma today," Kofi said. We all laughed. It seemed he hadn't gotten over Peabody's striking resemblance to his grandmother. "De colours of the Ashanti are at your back, Grandma."

We turned to look at the upholstered back of the chair in which Peabody sat.

"Are those really the Ashanti colours?" I asked.

"Yes, de green stands for our forest, de black for our people and de yellow for gold found in our land."

"Would you believe that the Jamaican flag has the same colours? I don't think the colours stand for the same things though."

We had moved leisurely through the tour and at the end we thanked Kofi for spending so much time with us and for his valuable information about some of our ancestors. We tipped him handsomely, but most significantly, Peabody gained a new "grandson."

As I looked around our host's spacious living room I could read Peabody's and Marie's thoughts. The day after tomorrow would be our last in Kumasi but no one wanted to discuss it. Afua served us cool lemonade, then sat in the sofa beside Peabody.

Peabody, unable to hold it back any longer, eased into the subject.

"My dear Afua, do you know of a driver we can hire to take us to Cape Coast when we leave?"

Afua turned to her and her eyes seemed larger and redder than usual.

"Yes, I have a driver that I use but I don't recommend you travel that way. It will be too costly. I suggest that you take the State Public Transport. It is safe and will get you to Cape Coast in about three hours."

Since arriving in Ghana, we had been chauffeured around by private car and hadn't used public transportation. I was interested in experiencing it first-hand.

"That's okay with us," Peabody said. "What time does the bus leave?"

"It leaves early each morning. I think you should buy your tickets today. I'll ask Akwasi to drive you to the bus depot to buy them."

I offered to go with Akwasi, allowing Peabody more time to bond with her old friend. Marie agreed to come along for the ride. At the bus depot we learned that the bus departed at 6 o'clock every morning.

Despite her grief and limited time to spend with her visitors, Afua drove us into town the day before we left Kumasi. We stopped to purchase goods from vendors in the street. We bought bananas, watermelon, oranges and vegetables. Although it was a Monday, the town bustled as it did the rest of the week. The streets were filled with

Nissans, Opels, BMWs and Toyotas, instead of Peugeots I'd seen during my previous visit.

Afua drove defensively into town as she maneuvered the traffic. Hundreds of people filled the streets: First, there were the women: women juggling huge enamel basins decorated with gaudy floral patterns on their heads; women balancing large bundles and other items such as baskets in their hands, and women holding toddlers' hands while they supported babies strapped to their backs. Then there were the men: men riding bicycles; men loading and unloading trucks in front of stores, and men carrying bundles. Along the sidewalks stood stacks of old tires, orange-painted drum cans and large bags the size of pillowcases stuffed with products. Amidst the foot traffic, cars, trucks, and buses laden with baggage in racks on top, whizzed by from every direction. Afua drove slowly along a crowded street, then switched to a narrow lane where she parked the car.

"Akwasi will pick up the car and take you all to do any last minute shopping you may have," she said as we piled out of the car.

"And what do you plan to do?" Peabody asked.

"I'm going to open my store for a little while."

She appeared so forlorn, I felt sorry for her. We trudged through the crowd, stepping on and off sidewalks as we came upon vendors with their goods spread out in our path. Afua led us toward a store, painted in blue and red.

"This is my store," she said, and pointed proudly at the building. But the proud look changed to anger almost as soon as it appeared.

"What on earth . . ."

Before she completed the exclamation, we realized why she was angry. A large pile of used clothing was stacked high in front of the store. A young woman, about seventeen, sat on a small rickety wooden stool off to the side of the pile. A toddler snuggled up beside her while she fed a baby in her arms from a bottle. The toddler wore a black and white patterned dress two sizes too large. It hung loosely over her protruding tummy, a sure sign of malnutrition. Her hair was braided and each braid had a coloured scrunchie. The child was very friendly and rushed over to us when I asked her name.

I watched Afua as she grappled with what to say to the intruder while trying to control her anger. She was a lady; I knew there would be no cursing. Finally, she moved close to the young mother.

"I don't mind if you're selling goods to make a little money," she said. Her voice was soft and she enunciated each word. "But for God's sake, you can't spread it out to block the entrance to my store, okay?"

"Sorry Ma'am, but de store was closed. I didn't tink it was going to open," the girl said.

It was as simple as that. You close your store while you grieve for your deceased brother and someone moves in and occupies the space in front of it. No questions asked and no fuss. It boggled my mind. As if she had all the time in the world, the young woman put the baby on a raggedy blanket on the concrete pavement. Then she pushed the pile of clothes toward the side. When a reasonable path was cleared, we entered the store behind Afua.

Inside, the store was crowded with pots and pans hanging from the low rafters. I wondered how Afua or her staff could find anything in the store. It reminded me of the old days in Jamaica when haberdasheries were cluttered with every conceivable item. Despite the jumble it was obvious that paint was the main product; rows of paint cans occupied several shelves.

We didn't have much to do so we hung around in the store with Afua. Only a few patrons came in. It seemed they didn't expect the store to be opened. Later, we learned from Afua that her sister-in-law severely reprimanded her for having the audacity to open the store before her dead brother was buried. Poor Afua had made a monumental error even if it was only for a few hours.

Akwasi arrived within the hour and we were relieved to see his handsome face. He was dressed in a pink shirt with buttoned-down collar and three-quarter length dark pants. The shirt wasn't tucked in and hung outside of his pants. We walked with him back to Afua's car. He drove us to Barclay's Bank where I converted more travellers cheques while Peabody and Marie converted some American dollars. A typical British Bank, Barclay's was organized and orderly, but the clerks moved as if tomorrow would never arrive. However, I didn't mind waiting because the building was air-conditioned. Outside the temperature was 33 degrees Celsius. As we exited the bank and headed back to the car, I noticed a man selling furniture at the side of the road. We strolled over to have a closer look. The furniture, a three-seater sofa with two matching chairs, was made from solid mahogany wood and well-crafted.

"What is the cost of the whole set?" I asked

"One million five hundred thousand cedis," the man said.

I did a quick mental calculation; at the going exchange rate, it was about $200 US. It was hard to fathom that such superior craftsmanship and quality wood – no particle board, no veneer – could be sold so cheaply.

Back in the car and out of earshot of the vendor, I turned to Akwasi.

"What is the minimum wage here?"

"It's 7,500 cedis a day."

"At least it has increased," I said. "When I was here five years ago it was 2,000 cedis per day."

"You're kidding me; 7,500 cedis is only one American dollar per day," Marie said.

Akwasi had no response for that. He changed the subject and made a suggestion.

"My bradas' store is just up de road; would yuh like to go dere?"

How could we say "no" to that? We knew what a visit to the store implied, but he had done so much for us, never complaining or hurrying. He stopped when we said "stop," took our pictures when we requested it, and he'd done whatever else we'd asked, and all in a pleasant manner. It would be the least we could do – patronize the family store.

"Sure, I would love to see the store," Marie said, excitement bubbling to the surface. Back home in Rochester she was the shopping queen. Marie's station in life was to eat, read and shop. Of course, she interspersed heavy doses of laughter for good measure.

"I'm sure we'll find something there," Peabody said.

Akwasi smiled, turned the car towards the south and in seven minutes he was leading us along a congested street into a tiny hole-in-the-wall store. A sign above it read *General Merchants, Importers & Exporters.* Two men, slightly older than Akwasi, greeted us at the entrance. I knew immediately that they were his brothers; the resemblance was obvious.

"Welcome to our store," one brother said. "Look around, please."

The store was chock full of goods; clothes hung from the roof, the walls, and anywhere that space could be found. Despite bright sunlight outside, the inside was partially dark; there were no windows, only the entrance door. We could barely find space to stand.

The brothers were definitely salesmen.

"I hear yuh will be leaving soon," one brother said. "How about some dress material to take back home?" He showed us an array of materials already cut into certain lengths suitable for an outfit. This was a standard way of selling dress material in Ghana. The fabrics were of various colours and patterns and were folded and hanging in squares on a rack. The three of us bought beautiful dress materials. Marie added beads and trinkets to her purchase. Akwasi smiled all the way back to the car. We were pleased that we were able to patronize the family store.

"I have one last place to show yuh," Akwasi said while we climbed back into the car.

"Where to this time?" Marie asked. She had hurriedly sat in the front seat as she had done the last few times we'd been out. Now that our visit to Kumasi was coming to an end it seemed she had started to warm up.

"I will tek yuh to one of our universities."

"Good choice, Akwasi," I said.

I'm always interested in seeing the seat of higher learning. I instantly recalled my pleasant experience when I had visited the University of Lagos in Nigeria five years earlier.

Our car pressed through heavy city traffic, escaped onto some side streets and before long we entered the gate of The College of Art. We could see several large buildings in the distance. The campus grounds were huge. Thick green lawns covered most of the unused areas, which were dotted with shapely trees. Small flowerbeds and low hedges of croton and other shrubs were arranged along the front of some buildings. We passed several buildings as we drove on smooth, paved roads. We spotted the dorms easily—clothing hung from windows, balconies and anywhere students could access sunlight. Akwasi did not stop or suggest we enter any of the buildings and we did not ask him to. We were content to drive by slowly and observe. But when I saw a sign that said *Gift Shop*, I asked him to pull over. An imposing Poinciana tree with large above-ground roots grew close to the store. Only a few of its exotic red flowers remained on the branches. Long brown pods of seeds, the final stages of the flowers, now hung from the branches. It was a spectacular tree. Marie and Peabody posed beneath it and I played photographer.

We entered a quaint little shop and an old man as black as charcoal, face glistening in the heat, looked up.

"Come in Sistahs, come in," he said.

He was about five feet and bald at the front. He wore a beautiful wine-coloured African garb, punctuated with pink swirls, leaving his right shoulder bare. As we inspected carvings, painting, crafts and other paraphernalia, he began to tell us about himself.

"I'm chief of my village," he said.

"Oh really?" I said. I didn't care if he was chief or king for that matter, but it seemed being a chief was a big deal in Ghana.

"If you're a chief what are you doing in the store?" Peabody asked.

"I just do dis part-time."

"Is your village near here?" I asked.

"Oh yes, not too far."

A small wooden plaque was nailed to the wall in the centre of the room. Carved into the wood were the words, "Come to me, Mathew 11:28." Peabody and I read the words simultaneously and laughed at the connotation. It was a popular occurrence to see written quotations of passages from the Bible placed on buildings in parts of Ghana. It seemed many who were Christianized took passages of scripture literally and felt that by putting these quotations on their cars and places of business that they would be blessed. I recalled two other passages I'd seen on shops: "Give all to God" and "Jesus is the key to my success."

I looked around the shop to see if anything was worth purchasing, something Ghanaian, something original. I spotted a darling painting of a mother and child; it was leaning against a wall, partially hidden behind another painting. I asked Chief to retrieve it so that I could look at it more closely. When he handed it to me I couldn't believe its condition. It was covered in several layers of dust. The canvas was a piece of cloth tacked onto a thin wooden frame that was falling apart, the nails grinning like a Cheshire cat. But something about the painting captivated me. The mother was dressed in a blue and white floral dress with a matching headscarf. She wore white beads around her neck and on both wrists. She was sitting on a chair. One round, firm breast was exposed and the baby cuddled in her arms, naked except for a white diaper, was sucking on it. The painting was passionate; it was dramatic; it touched me deeply. I asked Chief for the cost. By now I'd learned that you never accept the first price offered, so we haggled back and forth until I was satisfied with a price. When I returned to Toronto, the painting endured a magnificent transformation. The manager of the frame shop said he had to vacuum the material to remove all the dirt. He stretched the canvas, removed the old tattered frame and replaced it with a charming blue frame. It is fabulous and has become one of my treasured pieces.

Chief knew a tourist when he saw one and he was determined to have us unload some of our Yankee dollars before we left the store.

"Ma'am, look over here, look at dese sandals, yuh all should buy one."

Our eyes followed the direction of his pointing finger to a wall covered with sandals of every description. They were some sort of thong, made from leather; they all seemed oversized.

"I don't think any of those could fit us," Peabody said.

"Oh yes Ma'am, you try dem on den I nail down de strap to fit. Don't worry 'bout the width, we wear dem wide. We call dem *ahenema*."

Akwasi explained that the ahenemas were originally made wide for kings and queens so that they would walk slowly. We tried on several pairs in different styles and colours, and selected the ones we liked. Chief nailed down the straps to fit us. The three of us left the store with sandals and art. A happy Chief stood at the door grinning, still holding his little hammer in his hand.

On our way back to Afua's home Akwasi turned off onto a side street.

"My madah lives near here. I would like to take yuh all to meet her," he said sheepishly.

"That's so nice," I said. "Sure we would love to meet her."

Before long we arrived at his mother's home. A high fence enclosed the property. A large house was under construction, but the family was living in a small, older building at one side of the property. The mother greeted us at the door and invited us into the house. She was about fifty and seemed to be in good health. Several children ran around while we sat, chatted with her and drank the pop she served us. They were her grandchildren, she explained, the offspring of her six children. Akwasi was the youngest.

NINE

ROAD TRIP TO CAPE COAST

MARIE AND I jumped out of bed at the second blast by the muezzin the next morning. For the first time he was helpful to us. We showered, dressed and threw our last-minute toiletries into our suitcases. I walked out to the balcony and took a final look at the rambling city of Kumasi. A dull pink streak smeared the sky in the east. A slight glow lurked furtively behind the clouds. The sun would arrive in another hour or so. Yes, we had enjoyed a marvellous activity-packed time in the land of the Ashanti people. I returned to the bedroom and collected my suitcases. Marie was ready.

Cautiously, we carried our luggage down the stairs – it wouldn't be prudent to break a leg at this stage of our visit. I locked the door of the duplex behind us. We couldn't scale the wall as we'd done everyday since we arrived in Kumasi because of the heavy suitcases. We dragged our luggage down the walkway (thank goodness for wheels), opened the gate and walked along the road to Afua's abode.

I knocked on the front door several times before Afua opened it; she was still tying the sash of her robe. She'd obviously slipped it on hurriedly; it was turned inside out.

"My, it's you! What are you doing up so early?"

"We thought we should get moving once we heard the blaring at the mosque," I said.

"No one at this side is up yet," Afua said.

We knew our arrival would spur the household to action. Saywa trudged down the stairs with sleep in her eyes, but in no time she had breakfast ready.

The three travellers ate a quick breakfast while Afua went to call her neighbour, Sam. I had only seen Sam once since we arrived in Kumasi, when Afua introduced him to us. He was Akwasi's oldest brother. We had said our goodbyes to Akwasi the previous night and he'd been all choked up. Sam loaded some of the luggage into his car and placed the rest inside Afua's trunk. In convoy we headed for the bus depot. When we arrived, we found a long queue of passengers boarding the bus. Our tickets were clearly numbered and we assumed that seats were assigned; we saw no need to hurry. It was only a matter of getting on board.

Afua had been a great host despite the death of her brother and her inability to take us around personally. We took our time to savour our last moments with her. Peabody tearfully bade goodbye to her friend; the friendship had received a massive dose of reinforcement. After that Marie and I took turns to say goodbye to a lovely Ashanti woman – Afua Bonsu. My cousins and I were among the last six passengers to board the bus. When we entered all the seats at the front were taken. Peabody and Marie walked toward the back of the bus. But as I followed, I spotted the only vacant seat three rows from the front and promptly flopped into it. My derriere had barely touched the leather when someone tapped me urgently on my right shoulder. I swung around.

"You can't sit there," a white woman said, scowling at me. A sea of white faces, ruddy and sunburned, glowered at me from the front of the bus as if I was an alien.

"Why not?" I asked. "The seat isn't taken."

At that moment, a white man stepped into the bus.

"It belongs to him," the woman said, pointing.

"So where do I sit?" I stared behind me and could feel my chest tightening. "My number is C25."

I realized then that the number on the ticket meant nothing. Seating was on a first come, first serve basis. I couldn't understand why all the front seats were occupied by white folks. Was it deliberate? Was it an unwritten rule? Or had they just happened to arrive earlier than the black folks? I hoped the former two were NOT the case. I thought of arguing that I had every right to the seat, but noticed that all the black folks held their heads down and kept quiet. No one attempted to defend me. I decided to let it pass and gave up the seat.

A man near the back of the bus unfolded a seat in the aisle and beckoned to me. "Come Sistah, sit here."

I quickly took the seat and observed that the full length of the aisle had similar folding seats. Peabody and Marie had already secured one each. The bus, filled to capacity, pulled out shortly after. The aisle seat was low. I didn't have the comfort of the high back that the regular seats had to support my upper torso, but it was fairly comfortable except when the bus hit several potholes along the way.

The sun rose slowly, lazily, in the east as the bus snaked its way toward the south. Several passengers fell asleep, no doubt tired from waking up early to catch the bus. The landscape along the way to Cape Coast was mainly flat. Emerald flora unfurled around us everywhere. The valleys were hazy, covered in mist that had formed overnight. The driver floored the gas pedal and we zoomed through several towns and villages. I was convinced he was driving 130 kilometres an hour.

After 90 minutes, the driver brought the bus to a grinding halt at an outdoorsy restaurant in the town of Assintoso.

"This is a pee-pee stop," he announced. "We will be here for 15 minutes. Make sure you are back on the bus in 15; I don't plan to wait for anybody."

It was here in Assintoso, Ghana, that I discovered the female urinal.

Following closely behind some of the ladies from the bus, I entered what I thought was a washroom, only to find that there were no toilets or sinks behind the wall. The stall had a concrete floor, and built into the floor along the back wall, was a shallow gutter. I looked around flabbergasted. What had the women ahead of me done? There was liquid flowing in the gutter. Oh my God, they urinated in the gutter! But how did they do it? It was bad enough to have to squat, but how did I shoot it into the low narrow gutter? I tried a few poses, aware that if I didn't do it right, urine would be running down my legs. I looked around and realized that there wasn't tissue to wipe and even if there was where would I deposit it? With my jeans bundled around my ankles, I retrieved a tissue from my handbag and did my best to assume the position! The tissue came in handy to also wipe my legs! On my way out I passed Peabody in the queue waiting her turn.

"Make sure you have tissue," I whispered in her ear and gave her a wicked grin.

Another dilemma struck me when I returned to the courtyard.

I saw no evidence of water to wash our hands. Marie and I waited for Peabody to return, then I took my small bottle of drinking water from my tote bag. Using the precious liquid gingerly, the three of us washed our hands.

"Can you believe that urinal in there?" Marie asked.

"I've never seen anything like it before," I said. "I hope we won't have to use another one; my legs got in the way!"

"Mine too," Peabody said. We laughed knowingly. "Chalk it up to experience in Africa."

True to his word, the driver was ready in 15 minutes and we continued the journey south. As the sun climbed higher, the mist in the valleys evaporated. We arrived in Cape Coast to a bright, sunny morning. Because we didn't have hotel reservations, our first order of business was to find accommodation. While Marie and Peabody stood guard over our luggage at the bus terminus, I walked out to the road. I approached a man who was selling food at a small stall.

"Excuse me, sir, could you give me the name of a good hotel in the area?"

"Try the Golden Stream."

"Where is it?"

"Is around the corner," he said pointing to his left.

"Thank you very much."

Several taxis were parked at a stand a few metres from the terminus. I walked toward them. Three men jumped out of their cabs and swarmed me like vultures ready to pounce on a dead carcass.

"Take my taxi, Miss," one said.

"I'll take you, Miss," said another.

""My taxi is big enough," said the third man.

They had probably watched us as we alighted from the bus and collected our luggage.

I raised my hands in annoyance. "Okay, okay, I need a big car, more like a station wagon. There are three of us and we have six pieces of luggage."

They argued back and forth, all offering to take us, knowing full well that with our suitcases we could not possible fit into their taxi. I noticed a station wagon a little further along and walked over to the driver. He agreed to take us.

Golden Stream was a pristine, two-storey hotel. The receptionist seemed keen to do business with us.

"May we see one of your double rooms?" I asked. I always inspect hotel rooms abroad before I make a commitment.

"Sure Ma'am." She collected a bunch of keys hanging from a hook behind her. "Come with me, please."

"You go ahead and check it out Yvonne; I'll go with your decision," Peabody said. I saw tiredness etched on her face. She just wanted to rest.

"All right. Marie, please stay with your mom, okay?"

"No problem," Marie said.

I left them in the lobby and followed the clerk up two flights of stairs to the second floor. The room was large with a king-sized bed, beautiful drapes, and a TV. Watercolour paintings on the walls were easy on the eyes. The bathroom appeared sterile. An air-conditioning unit installed at the bedroom window, was turned off. She switched it on immediately.

"It's a nice room," I said to the clerk as we descended the stairs on the way back to the lobby.

"Yes, Ma'am, hope you'll take it."

"The room looks okay," I said to Peabody.

"Good."

I told the receptionist that we would take it.

"You'll need two rooms," she said.

"No, we do not need two rooms; we would like to stay together."

"Sorry Miss but it's hotel policy that only two persons can stay in a room."

'We don't mind paying extra for three if that's your concern, but we only want one room. If you can't give us that we'll have to seek accommodations elsewhere."

It was now mid-morning, and being diabetic, Peabody had to eat. She called me aside.

"Listen Yvonne, find out if we can get some food. Then we can work out the accommodations later."

I turned back to the clerk. "Can we at least get some breakfast now?"

"Sure Miss, just follow Mina upstairs and she'll fix it for you."

Mina, a young woman about nineteen, had been standing in the lobby watching and listening to us since we arrived.

I gave the receptionist a stern look. "I want to see your manager about the room. Is he in?"

"Not right now Miss, he usually comes about ten; he should be here soon."

"Okay, we'll go have breakfast. You let him know the moment he comes in that some potential guests would like to speak to him."

Mina fixed us a delicious breakfast of scrambled eggs, toast with jam and tea. Peabody had wilted like fresh cut flowers left in the sun without water, but after her first serving of breakfast she recovered and seemed perky like a new rose. I was sipping my second cup of tea when a middle-aged man strode into the room. He was clean-shaven and neatly dressed with his shirt tucked meticulously into tailored slacks.

"Hello ladies, somebody wanted to speak to me?" He looked inquiringly at us.

"Are you the manager?" I asked.

"Yes, I'm Charles Ansah, the manager and owner. Can I help you?" His voice softened.

"Hello Charles, I'm Yvonne. We are three ladies travelling together. We are strangers here and we would like to stay together. Your clerk says it's against hotel policy for three persons to stay in a room. Just let us know if this stands and we'll go somewhere else."

Charles scrutinized me from head to toe then broke into a big smile. "No problem at all, Yvonne, you can all stay in one room if you like."

"Thank you. That was easy."

"I always like to please my guests. Where are you folks from?" He had a mild accent.

"I'm Canadian and these two ladies are my cousins. They're Americans."

"Nice to meet you all. Welcome to Cape Coast."

Charles gazed into my eyes. "I tell you what, I'll even take you ladies around and show you Cape Coast."

Did I hear right?

I stared directly back at him. He seemed serious.

"And why are you being so kind to us?" I asked. From past experience I knew Ghanaians are one of the kindest, most hospitable people, but why would this businessman want to take us around? Maybe he wanted to make some extra money? He must have read my mind.

"It would be my pleasure to show you my town, no strings attached and no charge."

"That is really nice of you Charles," Peabody said.

He handed me his card. "Here is my number. My office is downstairs, across from reception. Just call me whenever you're ready to go out; I'll be available."

"Thank you Charles. You are very kind."I shook his hand. He clasped mine firmly; then he left the room.

TEN

CAPE COAST SLAVE CASTLE

I RARELY TURNED down a good offer, and considering our limited time in Cape Coast, I accepted Charles's offer. I telephoned him as soon as we'd settled into our hotel room and freshened up. We met with him in the lobby.

"So, where would you like to go first?" he asked, looking at my cousins and me.

I mentioned that we planned to spend two days in Cape Coast, so we could fit in trips to the Elmina and Cape Coast Castles. Charles made it clear that there were many other attractions to see and that we must visit Khakum National Park and walk The Canopy Walkway. . . .

Five years earlier, my first journey to Ghana had been a wonderful spiritual experience. Many of the moments will remain indelibly in my mind. But I'd refused to visit the slave castles, not because I didn't want to learn more about the slave trade; I didn't want to experience anything unpleasant, anything that would tarnish my memories and ruin my enjoyment. Now I was prepared to handle the ordeal.

Nonetheless, it had been a tough decision. Most people of African heritage who visit Ghana make the castles their primary tourist destination. Because I was unsure if I would ever be able to make the journey a second time, it would have been prudent to visit the castle, but I resisted. After my return to Toronto, friends had asked indignantly, "How could you go to Ghana and not visit at least one slave castle?"

I've revisited that decision often with ambivalent feelings. I would think I had made a mistake or console myself with Grandmother Eliza's wise words, "Nothing happens before its time."" In my heart I knew that someday I would return. Now here I was, thrilled to be back in Ghana. A visit to Cape Coast Slave Castle wouldn't be denied.

"Cape Coast Castle is our primary interest," I said.

"Okay," Charles said. "I'll take you there first, then we will have lunch. Tomorrow I'll take you to Khakum Park and afterwards I'll drive you over to see Elmina Castle. How does that sound?"

"I can't tell you how grateful we are Charles. Are you sure you have time to take us to these places?"

"Don't worry, if I didn't have the time I wouldn't offer. I have a few errands to run this morning. I'm building a new house. You know how it is; I have to keep an eye on the workmen. I'll drop you off at the castle and pick you back up around 1 o'clock, then we'll have lunch."

Charles spoke perfect English with a mild accent. I suspected that he'd lived abroad for a few years.

"Sounds good to me," I said, enthusiasm heavy in my voice.

We walked out to the front of the hotel and Charles left to bring his car around. I surveyed the area. Immediately to the left stood a large two-storey building. At first I thought it was another hotel, but when I saw a black man in his undershirt standing at a balcony watching us, I realized it was a private home. Across the street from the hotel two houses were under construction. They were two-storey mansions with Spanish-style arches and sturdy concrete balconies.

Charles pulled up in front of the hotel in his shiny black Opel and we piled in. I sat in the front. Charles turned out to be one of the kindest persons I've ever met. He assumed the role of tour guide and took us all over Cape Coast during the next three days. Yes, we decided to spend an extra day.

Charles drove along the streets of Cape Coast, through the main town and toward the coast. It was a unique town and much different from all the other Ghanaian towns I'd seen. Roundabouts, a typical road structure used by the British, were popular. It seems that in every country the British colonized you can find roundabouts. Charles pointed out landmarks. In the heart of town, a statue of a huge crab stood at a crossroad. It was the town's symbol. Further along from the intersection, he pointed out a nightclub.

"If you want to enjoy some of our nightlife, I could take you to that club over there; it's the *Blue Cheese.*"

Night life in Cape Coast? Was he talking to me? Blue Cheese sounds delicious!

"Of course I would love to." I turned to look directly at him, still wondering why he was being so kind. "Would you have time, though?"

"Yes, don't worry, I have time. How about 9 o'clock tonight?"

"You've got a date mister! Nine it is."

Peabody and Marie weren't nightclub folks; I knew I would be the only one on the date. I trusted Charles and was not concerned or afraid to be alone with him.

Wanting to learn about the place, I said, "I know each area of Ghana tends to have different tribes. Which tribe lives in this area?"

"Most of the people are Fanti."

"I assume you are one?"

"Yes, I'm Fanti," he said proudly.

We were near the coast. Charles drove slowly toward a tall gate. The building beyond was barely visible, but I knew we were at the place. My heart skipped a beat. We had arrived at Cape Coast Castle. Charles parked and led us to a small booth where he waited until we purchased tickets.

"Listen," he said to the three of us, "I won't be going on the tour with you, but I'll pick you all up for lunch, okay?"

"That's more than okay Charles; it's just great," I said. "Shall we meet you back here?"

"Don't worry, I'll find you in case I come back early." He left us at the ticket counter and returned to his car.

"The next tour starts in 45 minutes," the booth clerk said. "We have a small museum at one end of the building up the stairs; you're welcome to look at the exhibits until time for your tour."

We thanked her. With much anticipation we strode into the courtyard of Cape Coast Slave Castle. The magnitude of the structure jolted me. The castle was in fact a huge fort surrounded by high walls. The walls and the buildings were painted in white but it seemed the paint job had been done centuries ago. The walls were peeling all over and resembled a giant lizard shedding its skin. Stout black cannons were positioned through openings at intervals all along the retaining walls. I envisaged them years ago, poised, ready to pound any enemy coming from the ocean or the surrounding area. The fort was not built on a hill as most forts are built traditionally; neither was there a moat; therefore, attacks could have come from inland. But it was built right on the Atlantic Ocean, facing the sea, a strategic location good for defense and for shipping its disgusting cargo.

Many round cannon balls, the size of basketballs, were stacked in piles in the enclosed courtyard of the building. We walked across a cobbled stone courtyard and climbed several stairs to an upper floor where the small museum was housed. Moving along the rooms, we inspected artifacts, maps and bills of slave sales. We took photographs of interesting items. The history of slavery in Ghana was documented on black tablets posted around one of the rooms. I stopped to read some of the information:

The forced migration of Africans to the New World has been recorded as the major population movement in world history.... The extent of suffering that millions of enslaved people endured is beyond adequate description. Torn from their homes, families, separated from their children and loved ones.... The enslaved were shackled and held in dark dank unsanitary dungeons until they were shipped.... The conditions on board the slave ships were equally . . . .

The story was explicit and artifacts to prove it were displayed there. It wasn't a fairytale or a myth; it was real.

After exploring the museum we walked out onto the upper courtyard. I heard the roar of waves and moved over to the back wall. Before us, as far as the eye could see, was the Atlantic Ocean, wide and endless. To the left, near the beach, a few large houses, enveloped by tall palm trees, were barely visible. Immediately beyond the castle, little canoes loaded with fishermen bobbed in the ocean. Some of the fishermen sat on the beach and mended their fishing nets. Children played tag with the waves; they ran in and out of the water, squealing with laughter. The area had become a fishing village.

Do they have any idea about what transpired within the walls of this building many years ago? Do they know about the agony and suffering that their ancestors endured here?

I checked my watch. Time was up.

The building had several sets of stairs. We descended the closest one and joined the touring group. Ours consisted of 11 people: six whites and five blacks including my cousins and me. The guide was a sturdy Ghanaian, black as ebony. He was middle-aged, medium built and dressed in beige slacks and a black shirt with white patterns. His shirt was tucked neatly into his slacks. When he spoke his accent was so pronounced and his enunciation so off the mark, that several times I missed what he'd said. I'd rarely used my portable tape recorder since arriving in Ghana, but not wanting to miss the guide's valuable information, I whipped my recorder out from my tote and turned it on. I hoped that when I replayed the tape, I would be able to decipher it. Unfortunately, I was only able to understand about a half of the talk.

The guide led us to all the key areas of the castle, giving us a good sense of what the slaves endured during their incarceration. That's what it was; incarceration in the big white house as the white masters waiting for the white-sail ships to arrive to transport the black slaves to the unknown – the New World.

When he ushered us into a tiny, dark abbess, a room no more than 10 x 10, at the bottom of the castle, I knew this was the place that so many had visited, where so many had swooned, so many. . . .

ELEVEN

THE DUNGEON

I CAN STILL smell the funk. It is an odour you've never smelled before, nor will ever smell anywhere else. Musty and dank, the dungeon has retained this stench although more than two centuries have passed since the last inmates occupied the space in that tiny room. The malodour lingers, protecting, masking untold horror stories. It's the combination of urine forced from bladders when they could no longer contain it; of dried blood spilled by women merely for being born in a certain place, at a certain time, and having a certain skin colour; of tears shed from fear and pain; of sweat oozed from bodies in sweltering heat; of feces expelled when sphincter muscles could not hold it back, and of vomit spewed from regurgitated food that African slaves were forced to eat. Five years later, after making the journey to Cape Coast Castle, that smell has remained with me and will probably do so until I die.

As I stood in the dungeon, five years after my first visit to Ghana when I had opted not to visit the castle, it felt surreal.

"This is where the women were held," the guide said. "Sometimes as many as 150 of them were cramped into this little room. They would wait here until the ships came, sometimes for three months." He pointed to the dirt floor, and although the temperature was 32 degrees Celsius and bright outside, I could barely see it. "They had no toilets, no water to wash and no light except what came from up there."

The guide pointed to a tiny aperture at the top of one corner (I wouldn't grace it with the word "window.") "That tiny window would cast a little light when the sun was up."

I looked down at the dirt floor and noticed a rough channel down the centre. It was used to carry away the feces, urine and any other waste.

A male slave called Quobna Ottobah Cugoano who was sold to white traders for a gun, a piece of cloth and some lead, wrote an account of his experience in one of the dungeons. He stated it poignantly: "To conduct us away to the ship, it was a most horrible scene; there was nothing to be heard but rattling of chains, smacking of whips, and groans and cries of our fellow men. Some would not stir from the ground when they were lashed and beaten in the most horrible manner."

I looked around the room in the semi-darkness. As the funk penetrated my nostrils, my head began to expand until it felt like a huge Jack-o'-lantern pumpkin. I lost track of the guide's words. Instead I visualized scared, terrified women – some virgins, some mothers who had young babies to take care of, some married but not yet mothers, some with husbands and older children to attend to, all thrown together in this disgusting, claustrophobic place, waiting to be shipped to another world totally alien to them. How in God's name could they pack 150 people into such a small space? How did they sleep? How did they live for weeks, sometimes months, without light, beds and washroom facilities?

Anger began to seethe within me; my body shook. The stench in the room became more pungent and I began to breathe in spurts. The dirt floor began to rise up toward me. The breakfast I had eaten earlier rose to my throat. I gripped Peabody's hand. I had to get out of there.

In a haze I heard the guide say, "Let us move on to where the slaves entered the ships." I had already left the room. He led the group to the base of the central courtyard, beyond the female dungeon we had just visited. Walking slowly behind the group, with Peabody beside me, I was able to breathe normally again and my stomach began to settle. We trekked toward the side of the castle that faced the ocean. A large archway enclosed a pair of huge, black double doors. Written in bold letters above the door were the words *DOOR OF NO RETURN.* At first it seemed like a catchy slogan, a cliché, but as I read the words again it became clear that it meant a lot more. Staring at the sign, I realized that it was a thoughtless, insensitive and callous statement.

The guide provided more information.

"The men were shackled and held in rooms similar to the one you just came from. They would be led through an underground passage or tunnel and the women through another. They all met up here." He pointed to the door. "The ships arrived from England and were docked right on the ocean outside. The slaves were taken by boats to the ships, never to return."

Watching the guide mouth the words he had memorized so well, words he repeated several times each day, each week, I wondered if he felt any of the distress and anger that I felt at that moment. He swung the doors open and an "Ahhhhh" escaped from the group. Voluminous billows of the mighty Atlantic rolled in, splashed, then receded. The guide didn't have to explain farther. I could vividly envision the ships waiting, the cannons encased in the walls of the castle, pointing at the beach and at the backs of slaves shackled like animals, trudging along one by one toward the ship that would take them away. The logo above the door of the castle spoke an unequivocal truth. Once they trudged through that door, there was no return.

"Do you get a lot of tourists here?" a Caucasian member of the group asked. He was probably trying to break the sombre mood that had settled over us.

"Many foreigners come down here but they are mostly African-Americans or Africans from the Diaspora," the guide replied.

The guide was well rehearsed and he rattled off more facts, giving us little opportunity to ask questions.

"Cape Coast Castle became the second largest slave trading post in the world. It was originally built by the Dutch as a small trading lodge in 1630. The Europeans were always fighting for territory and later the Swedes captured it. But finally the British captured it in 1664. They rebuilt it between 1757 and 1780 and used it as a government house for colonial administration until 1877 when they moved their government offices to Accra, the present capital of Ghana."

"Are there more castles like this?" Marie asked.

"Oh yes. There are 42 European castles that were used as dungeons for millions of slaves. About thirty of them, including this one, are now recognized by UNESCO as World Heritage Monuments. The Elmina Castle is another famous one. It's only a couple of hours drive from here."

After the official tour, my cousins and I strolled around the castle on our own and took photographs. We visited the gift shop and bought post cards and souvenirs. Charles returned and found us in the souvenir shop.

"You ladies finish your tour?" he asked. "Was it good?"

"Let's put it this way, Charles, there is nothing good about slavery." I was sorry after I said it but I was still angry and upset.

"Sorry, wrong choice of words. Did you find it informative?" He stared at me with dark brown eyes as if reading my thoughts.

"Sorry, Charles, I didn't mean to snap at you. We learned a lot; it's just hard to take."

"Many tourists feel the same way." He pushed the thought aside. "Before we go for lunch I want you to meet the man who runs the small library here."

Charles took us to the library and introduced us to the gentleman. I had brought a couple of copies of my book, *Into Africa a Personal Journey*, the story based on my first journey to West Africa. I presented the gentleman with a copy and we posed for photographs. He was delighted with the gift and asked for my mailing and e-mail addresses. A few months after I returned to Canada and had forgotten about the man at the library, I received a letter from him asking for help to produce some brochures.

Charles took us to a rustic restaurant next door to Cape Coast Castle. A waiter greeted us and led us toward a table.

"Give us a table near the window," Charles said.

The waiter obliged and offered us a table close to an open window overlooking the Atlantic Ocean.

"What would you ladies like to drink?" the waiter asked. He turned to Charles.. "And you, sir?"

"Do you have fruit punch?" Marie asked.

"Yes, Miss."

"I'll have some."

"I'll have the same," I said.

"Let me have a beer," Charles said.

"Ice tea for me please," Peabody said.

The waiter returned promptly with our drinks and menus.

"What's good here, Charles?" I asked, scanning the menu.

"If you love seafood, this is the place. Everything is good but you might want to try the snapper or grouper. I'm not eating, so go ahead and order."

"Lunch is on us, Charles. I'm having the snapper, why don't you have it, too?" I asked.

"Thanks, but I don't eat a heavy meal at lunchtime."

I could see why; he was slim and lean, all muscles.

As we sipped cool drinks, I leaned back in my chair and looked at the shimmering turquoise body of water. It stretched endlessly. To the left, waves slammed against a jumble of rocks several feet from the castle's wall, then receded to the ocean. The sun shone from directly overhead, bathing Cape Coast with its warmth. The sky was a clear blue and cloudless, a day for picnics and outdoor activities, for hiking and biking.

A troop of boys about ten years old came into view. Some wore bathing trunks, while others, who couldn't afford these, wore their undershorts. A young man about sixteen, wearing only bathing trunks, led the pack. Like a drill sergeant he showed no mercy as he marched the boys up and down the beach under the scorching sun. He slapped two boys who fell out of line and the sound of skin on skin echoed across the ocean through the open window. The rest of the group howled with laughter. After they were exhausted, the leader allowed them a quick swim in the ocean.

The carefree happy boys faded from view and disturbing images of the slave trade engulfed me again. As if it were a mirage, I pictured a large intimidating ship stealthily moving out into the ocean. Tall masks erect, white sails billowing, it pulled out of the quiet harbour with its cargo of African slaves – black men and women carted away from their homes without consent, leaving all that they knew and loved behind, forced to go to a land where they would become chattels and be treated like animals. It was the most depressing thought. The bold sign above the door in the castle had been blatant and naked; it encapsulated the destiny of the slaves. The Atlantic was vast and on those journeys across the *Middle Passage* it was men against nature, men in the form of slaves who could never win. Millions died before the ships reached their destination; the rest never returned. My ancestors and ancestors of blacks in the Caribbean, Brazil and the United States never saw their homeland again. Tears welled up in my eyes; the thought was too difficult to take. I turned away from the window. Charles must have sensed my sadness for he covered my hand on the table with his.

TWELVE

NIGHT ON THE TOWN

I DRESSED CAREFULLY for my night on the town, not too casual, but not too dressy either. I selected a red pants suit; the shirt had a low-cut back. I accessorized it with white beads, white earrings and wore sandals instead of the running shoes that I'd practically lived in since arriving in Ghana. I substituted my big handbag for a small evening purse. I'd worn my hair in a large braid wrapped around my head since arriving in Africa. I brushed the stray strands back into place neatly and patted on light make-up. Peabody and Marie watched me dress and teased me all throughout.

I was to meet Charles in the hotel lobby at 9 p.m. He was there, ready and waiting when I arrived. He looked at me from head to toe, then cracked a big smile.

"You look lovely, Yvonne."

"Why, thank you, kind sir," I replied. "You look rather dapper yourself."

He was dressed in a light-blue shirt, unbuttoned at the neck, black slacks and shinny black shoes. He wore a sports jacket over his shirt. He put his arm through mine and escorted me to his car parked in front of the hotel.

We drove in silence for a while. I was curious about one thing and decided to broach the subject at once.

"Charles, I hope it won't be a problem with you taking me out. I presume you are married?"

"Yes, I'm married, and no, it's not a problem. My wife doesn't go to clubs. How about you, are you married?"

"No, I'm divorced."

I had suspected he was married the moment we'd met, but I became more certain after he mentioned that he was building a new house.

We arrived at the square with the huge crab. The square was lit up and so too was the club *Blue Cheese.* Charles parked on the side of the street and we walked into the nightclub. It was already partially filled with patrons.

"This must be a busy spot," I said.

"Yes, and it's only Tuesday. On Friday and Saturday nights you have to come early to secure a seat."

Inside the club, the lights were dim. Charles held my hand as we walked around until he found an empty table. A waitress came over as soon as we sat down.

"Anything from the bar?" she asked, and looked directly at Charles.

He turned to me. "Ladies first. What would you like to drink, Yvonne?"

"I'll have a rum and coke with a twist of lime."

"Bring us one rum and coke and a beer," Charles told the waitress.

"Do you always drink beer?" I asked, recalling he'd ordered beer at the restaurant next door to Cape Coast Castle.

"Yeah, most of the time. It's light; I can drink a few with no problem."

The waitress returned with our drinks and we toasted each other.

"To your first night on the town in Cape Coast," Charles said.

"To you, Charles, for being such a kind and generous host." The more I thought about it the more I realized that he was behaving like a host but he really wasn't one. He was simply a nice kind-hearted Ghanaian.

After a few sips I surveyed the club. It was average, nothing fancy, with low square tables and regular chairs. The music was a mixture of African and western and played at a moderate decibel. At least I could talk to Charles without having to shout. Charles also looked around the club. He saw someone he knew.

"Excuse me for a minute; I see one of my nephews over the far side."

He walked over to the nephew's table, greeted him and brought him over to our table.

"Yvonne, meet Eddie, my nephew."

"Hello Eddie, nice to meet you." I said, as we shook hands. Eddie looked at me curiously and I knew he had questions, but Charles quickly put his curiosity at rest.

"Yvonne is a visitor from Canada. She's staying at my hotel. I offered to show her a little of our nightlife."

Eddie accepted the explanation, and smiled broadly.

"Eh, welcome to Cape Coast; have a good time."

He returned to his table shortly after.

"You handled that tactfully, Charles."

"Thanks. You know how it is; people get wrong ideas sometimes."

We chatted and listened to the music, sipping our drinks leisurely. Charles ordered a second round.

Later Charles said, "How about something to eat? You should be hungry by now."

Remembering his refusal to eat at the restaurant earlier, I said, "I'm a bit peckish, but I'm not eating if you're not."

"Okay, I'll have something."

"What do they have? I don't want anything too heavy so late."

"I'll get a menu."

He left to find one. By this time the club was packed and all tables were taken. The patrons were a mixture of middle-aged and early 30s. The noise level raised a few more decibels. Charles returned with a waitress and a menu. I ordered chicken fingers and he chose the same. Within 10 minutes the waitress returned carrying hot breaded chicken fingers served in small bamboo baskets with carrot sticks tucked in one side. The chicken fingers were crunchy and tasty.

We ate, drank and chatted about Cape Coast and Canada. Just as I had suspected, Charles had lived abroad, in England, for several years. I enjoyed his company throughout the evening and was glad that I had accepted his offer to see a bit of nightlife in his town.

On the way home Charles stopped at another club located close to the beach. It was an open-air club with the bar elevated on a small hill. Tables and benches stood on lower ground, anchored between trees, a short distance from the beach. It was late and only a few patrons remained. Charles ordered drinks and while we waited, we sat on a bench and listened to the waves lapping and watched the stars glimmering through the trees. A cool wind blew off the ocean and caressed my bare back.

"Ooh, its cool out here," I said.

Charles quickly removed his jacket and placed it around my shoulders.

"Here, I don't want you to catch a chill," he said.

"Thanks. I don't think I'll catch a chill, but it's quite a drop in temperature."

"The wind off the ocean is always cool and refreshing."

Our drinks arrived and as we sipped them, we talked about ourselves. Hand in hand, we strolled along the beach, losing ourselves in the mystique of the night. Calm and serene, the gentle lapping of the waves, the salty smell of the ocean, and the indigo sky, dotted with glimmering stars, made it a beautiful night for lovers. It had been a long time since I'd felt so at peace in the company of a gentleman, for that was how my escort behaved all evening. But all too soon Charles had to settle the bill and we drove back to my hotel. He escorted me into the hotel to my door and made sure I was in safely before he waved goodnight then turned to go to his home.

The next day, Charles didn't wait for us to call. He offered to take us sightseeing. First he whisked us to Hans Cottage Botel for breakfast. The restaurant was one of the quaintest I had ever seen. Built on stilts, it stood above and was surrounded by a man-made lake. To reach the building, we walked on a boardwalk built a few feet above the water. As we strolled on the narrow walkway, I saw movements in the lake. Live crocodiles waded in the water.

Peabody froze. "I'm not going in there," she said. "Get me off! Get me off!"

Charles consoled her. "Don't worry Peabody, they won't come into the restaurant; you're safe."

She grabbed Charles's hand and held on as if her life depended on it. Together they entered the restaurant. Few patrons were about and Charles selected a table that afforded us a good view of the premises. The restaurant was a round building with a peaked thatched roof. A large bar was erected at one end. A part of the floor was made from thick glass. We looked down and saw several fish swimming below. Naturally, if the crocodiles swam our way, we could've also seen them.

"This is quite a novel idea," I said to Charles.

"Yes, it's popular with the tourists."

"Not with me it isn't," Peabody stated.

"I'm not so sure I like it either, Mommy," Marie said. "What if the crocs go crazy?" She stared all around to make sure her words hadn't come true.

We each ordered Spanish omelets, a popular item on the menu, along with tea and toast. It was obvious to everyone that Peabody felt uncomfortable the entire time. We left Hans Cottage Botel as soon as Charles paid the bill. I thanked him and apologized for Peabody, explaining that she had a deadly fear of creatures like snakes and crocodiles.

Back in the car, Charles said, "I'm taking you to a small village called Efutu. It was the first village in Cape Coast. It will give you a good insight into village life in Ghana. I'll introduce you to the chief who is a friend of mine."

He drove for a while, then turned off the main road unto an unpaved track. The road was narrow and in poor condition. The car bumped and swayed until it could go no further. Some of the villagers spotted the car and came out to see who we were. Charles spoke to them in dialect and reported to us.

"The chief is not in; he went into town about an hour ago. They don't know when he's coming back."

"That's too bad; I never met a chief before," Marie said.

"Sorry, but we'll stop here later if we have time."

On the way to see more of the city of Cape Coast, Charles stopped at his church, St Mary's Anglican. Poised atop a hill, it was an old gothic structure probably built in the early 1800s. Solid walls, constructed from cut stones, it showed signs of having endured years of tropical weather. Intricate stained glass adorned the windows and a steeple several metres high towered above the roof. When we arrived, two men and three women stood in front of the building. They turned to greet Charles. He exited the car and spoke briefly to the group, then returned with one of the women.

"Excuse me ladies, this is Mrs. Ulah. I hope you don't mind, but she is coming with us; I'm taking her for an appointment at a school."

Before Charles said anything more, I spoke.

"Why doesn't Mrs. Ulah sit beside you in the front? I'll sit with my cousins." I got out of the car, ready to join Peabody and Marie in the back.

"Thank you, but you don't have to do that; I can sit in the back." Mrs. Ulah said in her African-flavoured voice. She was a stout woman dressed in multi-coloured traditional clothes.

"It's fine, please have my seat." I opened the back door and slid in beside Peabody.

Mrs. Ulah took the seat and turned to give me a toothy smile. Charles waived to the rest of the group in the churchyard and started the engine. As soon as we were off the church's premises, a heated argument erupted between Mrs. Ulah and Charles. They spoke in a *Twi* language used by the Fanti people, but every now and again Charles hissed his teeth and punctuated his argument with "stupid." Although I didn't understand their words verbatim, I got the gist that Charles was angry with the woman for something she'd done. This exposed quite a different side of him, divergent from the calm, gentle side I'd seen so far.

Charles drove a few miles then entered a wide iron gate. The path beyond led us up a steep hill to a large compound.

"Ladies, this is Mfantsipim School," Charles said as he parked at the end of the driveway.

The buildings were impressive, old and scholastic. Two boys barged out of one building and stood on a paved landing. They were neatly dressed in uniforms different from the ones worn by students we had seen along the streets of Ghana.

Charles stepped out of the car, then stuck his head through the passenger's window.

"I'm trying to get Mrs. Ulah's son into this school. I'm going inside with her. Please make yourselves comfortable. Feel free to walk around and stretch your legs until I come back."

"Goodbye ladies," said Mrs. Ulah.

We bade her goodbye and wished her luck. She had to trot to keep pace with Charles who walked away without as much as a glance at her. Peabody and Marie didn't budge, but I stepped out of the car and strolled around the immediate premises. Perched on a hill and tucked away from the hustle and bustle of the town, Mfantsipim School was nestled cozily among luxuriant vegetation. Birds chirped in trees and flew overhead. The air was fresh, the environment conducive and favourable to studying. No noticeable distractions were apparent.

Charles returned within twenty minutes without Mrs. Ulah. I joined him, regaining my spot in the front seat. He drove slowly down the hill.

When he spoke he was still fuming.

"One thing I can't stand is stupid people."

"Is Mrs. Ulah going to get her son into the school?" I asked.

"I don't know; I hope so for her sake. I told that woman weeks ago to come to Cape Coast and I would set up an appointment for her to meet a friend of mine at the school. She delayed and delayed, then last minute she arrives. It's not easy to get into this school. People from all over Ghana want their sons to go there; you need connections."

"What's so special about the school?" Marie asked.

Charles glanced over his shoulder at her. "The reputation is excellent. It's a private boarding school for boys, very strict. Some top-class students have come out of it. Kofi Annan attended this school. Everyone with money wants their sons to go there, but if you don't have connections it's not easy."

Isn't that the way of the world these days? Have money, buy anything.

After our exchange Charles calmed down and his mood changed. He metamorphosed back to the charming gentleman I'd come to know.

It was after our Botel crocodile experience, failure to meet a chief, and a quick stop at Mfantsipim School, that Charles took us to Kakum National Park and the adventure on the canopy walkway began. . . .

On the third day, my cousins and I prepared to leave Cape Coast. We had opted not to visit Elmina Castle. We planned to continue on to Accra by the State Transport Bus. Charles drove us to the bus terminus while a taxi followed with our luggage. The bus was scheduled to arrive at 10 o'clock. Charles waited patiently with us until it arrived. It trundled into the station at 11:15.

Despite the unpleasant emotions I'd experienced during my visit to the slave castle, I felt sad to leave Cape Coast. It had been a warm homely place, filled with mystery and wonder. Peabody and Marie shook Charles's hand, said goodbye and boarded the bus, leaving me to say farewell. Standing beside the bus, I gazed up at Charles. His face looked like a thunderstorm about to erupt. I fought back tears. I realized then, that we had become attached during the short visit. I promised him to stay in touch and we exchanged addresses. I pecked him on the cheek and boarded the bus. This time we found regular seats. Peabody and Marie sat together and I sat alone, but not for long.

A handsome, fair-skinned man with striking gray eyes and a body that had spent time in a gym, took the seat beside me. He introduced himself as Donald. We struck up a conversation immediately and it continued until we arrived in Accra some two hours later. A native of Sierra Leone, he had lived in the United States for many years. He was a professor at the University of Kentucky, but had been living in Ghana while on a six-month sabbatical.

I mentioned my Jamaican roots and Donald promptly pulled out his wallet. He removed a business card and handed it to me.

"Keep this card, Yvonne. This lady is a Jamaican who lives in Accra; I want you to contact her while you're in town."

"What is she all about?" I asked.

"She's a wonderful lady and very interesting. She knows me well. She'll put you in touch with Jamaicans living in Accra."

Unfortunately, time did not permit me to make the contact as we spent little time in Accra.

We became so absorbed in conversation that I was unable to concentrate on the landscape and missed most of the scenery. Occasionally Donald pointed out a landmark. He singled out Weija Lake, the lake that supplies water to the town, and McCathy Hills, an area just outside of Accra, where the upwardly mobile Ghanaian wants to live. Beautiful homes and villas dotted the hillside. Gazing at the homes I observed several of the trees with clusters of cup-shaped orange flowers in the valley. I assumed Donald, being highly educated, would know the name and help me to put the matter to rest.

"Donald, do you know the name of those flowering trees over there?" I asked.

He looked out the window and nodded. "Yes, the botanical name is spathodea. They are also called African tulip. You'll find them in my country and all over West Africa."

"Thank you so much. I've been trying to get that answer for days, but Ghanaians don't seem to know it."

We came upon a crowded market where an overhead bridge connected both sides of the street. Vendors selling fresh vegetables, oranges and a multiplicity of goods lined the street. Donald informed me that it was Kasoa Market and that on Tuesdays and Fridays it was so busy, it was impossible to cross the street.

That explains the overhead bridge.

By the time we said "goodbye" in Accra, we had exchanged telephone numbers and e-mail addresses.

THIRTEEN

YOU CAN'T GO BACK

WE TOOK a taxi from the bus terminus in Accra to Koby's Hotel. Lily, the half-Japanese receptionist, greeted us with a warm smile.

"*Akwaba*, welcome back. I'm so glad to see you all again."

"Thank you Lily," I said. "It's nice to be back."

"I will give you the same room you had before. Is that okay?"

"That will be just fine."

Ken, Afua's nephew and the hotel's owner, barrelled out of his office to greet us. We were pleased to be his paying guests this time. He helped to carry our luggage to the room.

"There isn't much for us to do here and the evening is still young," I said to Peabody and Marie while we organized out toiletries." We would be spending only a night here.

"You have an idea," Marie said. "I can tell."

"Yes, I do." Mother and daughter stared at me, waiting. "Listen, I haven't had a chance to try to connect with any of the people I met in Ghana when I came here the first time. I want to visit Paloma, the hotel where I stayed, to see if some of the folks I met there are still around. Are you two interested in tagging along?"

Peabody showed enthusiasm as usual; she was always ready for an adventure.

"Of course I would love to," she said. "You're right; there's nothing to do here except to watch TV and I certainly didn't come all this way to Ghana to watch the boob tube."

Marie added her concurrence. "Count me in."

"Before we leave, let me try Paddy's number," Peabody said. "I haven't called him yet."

Paddy, a Ghanaian who lived in Accra, was the brother of a member of Peabody's church in Rochester. Peabody had given me Paddy's name and telephone number when I visited Ghana the first time. He had been my only contact when I arrived. Although I never met him until my last day in his country, through his connections, he'd been very instrumental in helping me to secure a visa to Nigeria. Using the telephone in the lobby, Peabody called Paddy's number. No one answered.

I advised Lily of our plan to visit Paloma; then we tramped through the potholes in the dirt lane until we reached Adenta Road. There we caught a taxi to Accra. The road into the city was strangled with rush-hour traffic. The cab travelled slower than a rickshaw driver in Beijing. Finally, the car turned a corner onto Ring Road. Vivid memories of the place and Adamson flooded my mind. I'm always amazed at how the mind can be readily stimulated to conjure up images when the senses work in tandem. My sense of smell transported me back to Adamson's Hugo Boss cologne. I could even taste the meals I'd eaten at the restaurant with the thatched roof at the Paloma Hotel complex.

The taxi driver deposited us at the hotel's gate. Paloma Hotel was the central part of a small complex. The buildings included a two-storey hotel, a few small shops, a restaurant and a cobbled courtyard. We entered the courtyard and I instantly saw changes. I led the way up a flight of stairs and walked over to the reception desk. I didn't recognize the man standing there.

"Good evening," I said.

"Good evening Ma'am; can I help you?"

"A few years ago I stayed at this hotel. There were some lovely people working here. I wanted to see if they're still around and say hello to them."

The man looked curiously at me. "What were their names, please?"

"There was a young man named Humphrey and a lady named Yvonne. Do they still work here?"

He shook his head slowly. "Sorry Ma'am, I've been here for two years now and I've never heard of them."

I smiled at him. "I took a chance that they'd be here. Thanks anyway."

On the way down the stairs Peabody said, "Nothing stays the same."

Human beings are creatures of habit. Most of the time we expect to see things the same way, to do things the way we did them before.

"You're right; the thing is, you don't mind if the change is for the better. Let's go see what's new at the restaurant and have some dinner."

Another surprise awaited us.

The restaurant at Paloma's complex had been unique and homely. Elevated above the courtyard, it had been surrounded by a low wall and opened at the sides. You could hear and watch the traffic zipping by as you dined. It had a high wooden roof covered with dried palm leaves; this had given it an African hut look.

I entered the restaurant to find it totally transformed. The open sides had disappeared; the entire restaurant was enclosed. You now watched the traffic through large glass windows. The roof was regular; the thatched roof no longer existed. The waiters previously had worn the customary black pants and white shirt. Now a group of young waiters milled about in blue jeans, navy blue golf shirts and little red aprons. Navy blue baseball caps completed their ensembles.

"This place must be under new management," I said. "They've revamped the whole place."

Our waiter brought us menus. They were also new. Some of the traditional Ghanaian dishes: kenkey, banku, balava and fufu remained, but several new items, tilapia, jolloff rice, pizza and falafel had been added.

Marie studied her menu, then rolled her eyes.

"Did you see the prices on the menu? A medium pizza is 39,000 cedis!"

"Okay Cuz, let's not get overly excited about the prices; remember you have to do the conversion first." I did a quick calculation. "It's just about $5 US. That's reasonable don't you think?"

"Yeah, you're right. I can't get used to the big numbers."

Marie remained very quiet during the meal.

After dinner we visited the little boutiques selling crafts and clothes in the complex. Paloma had lost its unique ambiance; unwittingly the change helped to deaden my memories of Adamson. There was one good thing about all this, however, the change seemed positive. I was disappointed at not being able to connect with anyone that I'd met on my first journey to Ghana, but as the saying goes, *que sera, sera.*

We caught a taxi back to Koby's. Rush hour had ended; the drive was much quicker than the outgoing one. Little chatter took place between the cousins; we were absorbed in our own thoughts. Peabody and Marie had learned much about Ghana with each day unfolding a new chapter. For me, the story continued with still more chapters to be revealed.

On our return to the hotel, I telephoned Pastor Ray. He promised to come the next day to take us to visit Tema.

FOURTEEN

THE PREACHER MAN

I WAS AS nervous as a bride-to-be getting dressed for the wedding ceremony. This kind of jittery unsettling feeling was almost alien to me. Having developed a thick skin over the years, few things fazed me. Yet, here I sat in Koby's Hotel lobby, packed and waiting for a man I knew little about, a man I'd never met. I had communicated with this man via e-mail for a year but we'd exchanged little personal information. Our e-mails mainly pertained to Frieda, my protégée.

He was Pastor Ray, a minister with a Pentecostal church in Tema. A few months earlier, in one of my e-mails, I'd mentioned that my cousins and I planned to visit Ghana and that I hoped to meet Frieda. He had pleaded with me to visit Tema and offered to put us up. I hadn't visited Tema on my first trip to Ghana and knew nothing about the area. I anticipated exploring it.

My nervousness amplified when my thoughts brimmed over with Frieda. Would she like me? Would I like her? Several months earlier I'd received two photographs of her, one from Pastor Ray, and the other from Anita Sinclair, the woman from North Carolina who'd told me about her. The photos showed a slender young girl with a big, infectious smile and hair cropped low like a boy's.

I was sitting in a wing chair in the small lobby, surrounded by our suitcases and hand luggage. They had been placed wherever there was space. Peabody and Marie had stepped outside, probably to have one last look around. Relax, I told myself, maybe we'll get along like bread and jam. Maybe she'll just open up and inundate me with conversation, telling me about school, her parents, her friends, and all the fun things that she did in Ghana. We'd corresponded by mail and later e-mail. In her second letter, she'd asked to call me Auntie Yvonne. I'd agreed without hesitation. Maybe she would pour it all out on her new Auntie Yvonne. Then I thought, if I'm an outgoing, outspoken, extraverted adult, and I'm so nervous, wasn't there a strong possibility that little Frieda would be just as nervous, or even more so?

Lily , the receptionist on duty, sat at her desk watching me. She smiled when I looked her way. She was a charming girl, about twenty. She was very fair with thick wavy hair and a flat face with high cheekbones. The previous night I'd been yearning for citrus and she'd offered to drive me up the long potholed-lane to the crossroad at Adenta.

"Lots of street vendors are at the corner," she had said. "You can buy oranges or grapefruits if you like."

"You don't mind taking me?"

"Oh, no; I need to buy something at the drugstore up there anyway, so I'll do it then," she said in perfect English.

At 7 p.m. it was already pitch dark. How nightfall seemed to descend almost suddenly upon Ghana always amazed me. Lily and I slipped into her tiny car and she negotiated the obstacle course they call a road, as we drove to Adenta. I took the opportunity to get to know her better.

"So tell me a little about yourself. You're obviously mixed."

"Yes, my mother is African, but my father is Japanese."

"Do you know him or see him?"

"No, I don't."

"What tribe is your mother from?"

"She is from the Krobo tribe; they live in Eastern Region."

"Anything special about them? I've never heard about this tribe." Then again, with some fifty tribes in Ghana, I hadn't heard about many of them.

"Oh . ... well they have their own dialect also called Krobo. They wear lots of beads all over their bodies. They wear it on their waist, their neck and their ankle."

I wanted to ask more questions, one being about female circumcision, but we arrived at Adenta Road. We entered the main road and I observed a red neon sign flashing, *Internet Café*.

"Hey Lily, do you mind if I go check my e-mail? I see an Internet place over there." I pointed to the sign.

"That's okay. The drugstore is below. We can meet in front when you're finished."

The café was on the second floor of a building that housed five or six other businesses. It seemed safe, brightly lit, and knowing that Lily would be waiting below, gave me some comfort. I bounded up the stairs and entered the café. The manager, a sturdy black man, stood like a bouncer behind the counter.

"Can I help you, Miss?"

"I would like to retrieve my e-mails."

"It will cost you 1,000 cedis for five minutes."

"That's okay. I might even need more time."

"Just let me know if you do and I'll give you more time. You just pay the extra."

I gave him 1,000 cedis.

"Use computer number three over to your right."

I moved toward the computer he indicated and sat down. There were six computer stations in the room and two were occupied. The machine made a few sounds as it booted up and soon I was able to access Hotmail. I began to read my e-mails but there were too many. Not wanting to waist money reading unnecessary mails, I quickly zapped the ones that looked like spam or ones that seemed unimportant to free up space. I sent a two-liner e-mail to my son and Delores, Peabody's middle daughter, informing them where we were and that we were having a great time. The computer was very slow and I ran out of time. I paid another 1000 cedis and read as many e-mails as I could.

I met Lily downstairs as agreed and she drove across the street to the lane and stopped beside a row of fruit vendors. Their little stalls were lit with kerosene lanterns. At that moment, bedlam broke out. It was as if a hawk had entered the chicken coop. Everyone began to shout and call out to us.

"Over here."

"Buy from me."

"I give yuh good price."

I quickly bought a dozen oranges from the nearest vendor. We dashed back to the car and headed back to the hotel.

I tried my best to remain calm as I waited in the lobby for Pastor Ray and Frieda to arrive. Peabody and Marie joined me. We peeled and ate a few of the oranges left over from the previous night. I was enjoying my second fruit when the phone rang. Lily said a few words into the receiver then called me to take it.

"Hello, this is Yvonne."

"Pastor Ray here. How are you? Enjoying your visit so far?"

Mmm, his voice was delicious. I was hearing it for the first time.

"I'm great. Just waiting here for you."

"I'm sorry, I'm going to be about thirty minutes later than I thought, but I'm on my way."

"That's okay. See you soon."

There wasn't much I could do. I appreciated that he took the time to call. The more I thought about Pastor Ray, the more I began to see him as a gentleman. When I'd mentioned to him via e-mail that I planned to visit Ghana, and would love to meet Frieda, he'd promptly offered accommodation. He mentioned that he shared a house with the senior pastor of his church and that there was room for my cousins and me. I countered that we were fine with staying in a local hotel, but he wouldn't hear of it. Not wanting to impose on him and the other pastor, I'd plan to spend only two days with them, just time enough to get to know Frieda.

I looked up from flipping through a magazine I'd purchased at Amsterdam Airport Schiphol when a six-foot-two, slim man walked into the lobby of Koby's Hotel. Our eyes met and he broke into a wide grin that lit up the room. He stretched his long arms out to me and I stood up and burst into a smile.

"Yvonne?" the man said. "Nice to meet you. I'm Pastor Ray."

"Pastor Ray, finally we meet," I said as we hugged each other.

The earth stood still. His touch was ever so gentle, as light as a peacock's feather. I instantly felt as if I'd known him for years. I'd expected someone older (He was about thirty-two.) but at that moment it didn't matter. I recovered from the surprise.

"Where is Frieda?" I asked. "You left her in the car?" I peered around him.

"Sorry, I didn't bring her with me. I wanted to leave space for you all and your luggage. We'll go to see her as soon as we reach Tema." He looked deep into my eyes and smiled again.

I was disappointed at not meeting Frieda, but I understood his reasoning. My anxiety dissipated.

Marie and Peabody heard the commotion and rushed into the lobby to meet our new host. I introduced them and Pastor Ray gave them both hugs.

"Pastor John, our senior minister, is outside in another car; I want you to meet him." There was a reverence and obvious respect in the way he alluded to his colleague.

He led us to a blue Toyota parked outside the gate of the hotel. Two men sat in it. One, a little older and shorter than Pastor Ray, stepped out from the passenger side and greeted us. When he smiled, two large front teeth protruded over his lip. It was hard not to stare at them; they were so conspicuous. Except for the teeth, he was a good-looking man. His hair was well-groomed and he wore a loose floral African shirt.

"Nice to meet you all," Pastor John said. "Welcome to Ghana."

"Thank you so much for offering to accommodate us," I said.

I wanted to get that in quickly. After all, we were total strangers. We'd never met; yet this minister did not hesitate to offer kindness. But by now I knew what Ghanaian hospitality was like; I'd experienced it on my first visit to Africa, and I'd experienced it with Charles Ansah. The kindness of the African people knew no bounds.

Pastor John was businesslike. "Look, we are late and I don't want it to get dark before we get to Tema. I'll take some of your luggage in my car and you can all drive with Pastor Ray so you can get acquainted."

The drivers loaded most of the luggage into Pastor John's car; a hired taxi. The rest we put into Pastor Ray's car, also a hired taxi.

We said goodbye to Lily and Ken, mentioning that on our return from Tema we planned to use the hotel again. Although Koby's was off the beaten track, I felt it was better to stick to what we knew. At least the service was good and we would be patronizing Afua's family.

FIFTEEN

TEMA

THE YOUNG man was handsome and decidedly "hot." Why was he a pastor in a church? I had learned via his e-mails that he was single. At 32, most African men were married with children. Now that I'd met Pastor Ray, I had a burning desire to know more about him.

But for the moment, sitting in the back of the taxi with my cousins, I decided to focus on the scenery. Chances were I would only pass that way once. We rode for several kilometres before we left the hustle and bustle of Accra. The driver, a middle-aged man, drove at a good clip, but carefully. The road was in very good condition, without potholes, unlike the lane we had travelled to and from Koby's Hotel. Verdant vegetation dispersed in patches between residential and commercial buildings kept nature always at the forefront.

I tapped Ray on the shoulder. "Can you tell us a little about Tema, Ray?"

"Sure. Tema is the most beautiful city of Ghana." He looked around at us and grinned exposing perfect white teeth. "Of course I'm biased. I live here!"

We laughed and encouraged him to continue.

"Tema is our port town; it is famous because it has the largest and most popular port in Ghana. It's not a natural harbour, though; it's manmade. It was opened in 1961. Tema is only about 25 kilometres from Accra."

"So what kind of cargo is handled there?"

"Most of the stuff we export passes through Tema harbour – cocoa is one, and timber, but it's not just the exports; industries like aluminum, oil refinery and building materials are also there. I'll take you on a tour tomorrow."

"That would be nice," Peabody said.

"What about the people who live here?" I asked. "I know different tribes tend to reside in different areas."

"Most of the people who live in southeast Ghana are Ewe. They're the same tribe in Togo and Benin."

"Oh really? I had a chat with one of the receptionists at Kolby's and she said the Ewes love to give their children names like Faith, Prudence, Hope and Charity."

"Yeah, they do. I guess it's from being Christianized."

"Those names certainly sound Christian to me," Peabody said.

As we entered the Tema region, I sensed a difference. It was a costal area and even the temperature was different.

Peabody suddenly yelled, "Stop! Let's get some coconuts."

She'd spotted a vendor selling fresh coconuts along the road. The driver stepped on the brakes and tires screeched, but we'd already passed the vendor. He reversed and stopped by the vendor's cart. We all eased out of the car. Ray spoke to the vendor in dialect and passed on information to us about the price. Peabody ordered coconuts for each of us and three additional ones to take to Tema. We drank the thirst quenching sweet water by the side of the road, then asked the vendor to cut the fruits open so that we could eat the white, milky flesh inside.

"It's as good as in Jamaica," Peabody said.

"Yes, brings back memories of the good old days doesn't it?" I said.

"It sure does. I can't understand why anyone would forget their roots."

With stomachs filled with coconut water and flesh, we returned to the car and continued our journey. We passed several churches along the road as we came closer to the town.

"Are there any Kingdom Halls near where you live?" Peabody asked.

"Yes, there is one close by. You could actually walk to it, but if you're going to attend service I suggest you take a taxi."

"Thanks. Can we stop there so I can check the service time?"

"No problem." Ray spoke to the driver and in few minutes we were winding our way along a driveway toward a building with a large sign that read *Kingdom Hall.*

Peabody and Marie went to search for the information. Thy tried the front doors of the Kingdom Hall but they were locked. Not a soul was in sight. A glass display unit was attached to the front wall. They peered inside and read the notices pinned there. One notice included the hours of services. Marie wrote down the information, then they returned to the car.

"Can you believe it?" Peabody asked. "They have three services on Sundays in three different languages - Ga, Twi and English. The English service is at 11."

"That's the same time as my church," Ray said. "I'll arrange a taxi for you tonight."

Always polite, Marie said, "Thank you, Pastor Ray."

While Peabody and Marie were Witnesses, I was not. I would therefore not accompany them to the Kingdom Hall. I planned to attend church with Pastors Ray and John.

We had only driven a short distance from the Kingdom Hall when Ray turned to us.

"We are almost there," he said.

We gazed at the road ahead, waiting to see our new abode for the next couple of days. I had accepted the invitation to spend a few days with Ray on blind faith. He hadn't described the accommodation and I hadn't inquired. The taxi pulled off the main road unto an unpaved narrow dirt road. Here potholes gaped at us; the earth was dry and thirsty. This seemed to be standard with the side roads. Not encouraging, I thought. The driver swerved in and out, around and about and finally pulled up at a wrought iron gate built into a low wall. A branch of an almond tree with large glossy leaves protruded over the wall.

Ray turned to smile at us, then made a grand announcement.

"We're home!"

We quickly exited the car and looked around to see the place that would be our home for two days. Beyond the low wall stood a row of 10 two-storey townhouses painted in delicate yellow with pink window and door trims. Small balconies on the second floor of each unit were made from decorative blocks painted white. The houses were attractive and appeared to be in good condition. Ray unlocked the gate and wedged it with a stone to keep it opened. The driver began to remove our suitcases from his trunk.

"Do you think Pastor John has arrived yet?" I asked.

Thoughts that the rest of our luggage may have been stolen began to percolate in my mind. Ray seemed to read my thoughts.

"He's not here yet. Don't worry. He probably stopped at the church. He'll be here soon with the rest of your luggage."

We entered the townhouse for the first time. It was average in size. The men put our luggage inside the house, in the hallway. Ray took out his wallet to pay the driver, but Peabody and I promptly objected. I paid the driver and he departed. Peabody asked that we hold hands and she said a brief prayer, thanking Jehovah for bringing us safely to Tema.

Ray invited us into the living room. It was furnished with an overstuffed brown sofa, two chairs, a bookshelf bulging with religious books, a coffee table and two end tables. A TV stood on a polished wooden stand against the wall in the centre. The room was cozy, but not luxurious.

A woman dressed in western clothes appeared from the back of the house and Ray introduced her to us.

"Ladies, this is Sister Alma; she attends our church. She helps us out with the cooking and so forth."

Sister Alma smiled and did a slight curtsy.

"Can you bring our guests some lemonade?"

Alma disappeared into the kitchen and returned almost immediately carrying a tray with tall glasses of lemonade.

Pastor John arrived moments after we'd settled down and drunk our lemonade. I finally relaxed when his driver placed the rest of our luggage in the hallway.

"Ladies, welcome to my home," Pastor John said. "I hope you will enjoy your visit with us. Ray, please show our guests their rooms."

He smiled and again the front teeth caught my attention. Why wouldn't he have done something about his teeth? I wondered. Was it a lack of money? Were no dentists available to do the job? Maybe he didn't see anything wrong with it; that I found hard to believe. One thing was certain, his body language and subtle choice of words made it clear that he was the boss.

"Okay ladies, I'll show you your rooms," Ray said. "Follow me please."

He led us up a steep staircase. A three-piece bathroom was immediately at the top of the stairs. To the right was a bedroom with a double and a single bed. The louvre windows were opened and I could see the backyard and the neighbours' houses that backed onto the property. To the left was another bedroom with a double bed. The bedroom to the left was the largest and obviously the master bedroom that belonged to Pastor John. The rooms were clean, the beds neatly made and covered with brightly coloured comforters.

"You can decide between the three of you which rooms you would like to occupy."

I looked and Peabody and signalled that I would speak.

"Ray, I think it is so kind of you and John to put us up and sweet to give up a bedroom, but the three of us can bunk in this room." I pointed to the room with the two beds.

"Are you sure? We have another bedroom downstairs that Pastor John and I can share. It's not a problem."

"We really appreciate the gesture, but one room will be just fine. Peabody and Marie will sleep in the double bed and I'll use the single. We'll be okay. Besides it's only for a couple of days."

"If you're sure, then it's settled," he said.

After we organized our toiletries, Ray offered to take me to meet Frieda. The excitement I'd felt in the airplane returned.

I'm going to meet Frieda finally!

Leaving my cousins behind, we walked a short distance from the townhouse to the main road. Ray hailed a taxi. We drove to the house of Frieda's aunt. On the way Ray talked about her.

"Frieda's mom works in the market. She works long hours. She usually leaves Frieda at the aunt's."

We were driving along a street with rows of small modest houses when Ray asked the driver to pull over. We stopped in front of a house painted pale blue. Ray stepped out of the car and banged on the gate several times. A middle-aged woman sauntered to the gate and spoke briefly to him.

Ray returned to the car.

"Sorry, Frieda isn't here; she's at the market with her mother."

"Are we going to the market then?"

"No. It's no point going to the market. Besides I'm sure you're tired. Frieda will come to church tomorrow. Pastor John and I will arrange for you to meet with her in his office before service begins. Okay?" He looked at me with apologetic eyes.

"Sure."

What could I do? I was disappointed at not meeting Frieda for the second time, but I supposed an extra day wouldn't hurt. We returned to the townhouse.

SIXTEEN

FRIEDA

THE TOWNHOUSE bustled with activity on Sunday morning. Five adults showered – we never worried about a shortage of hot water – we didn't need it. Five adults performed their individual brand of toileting and dressed for Sunday service.

Ray and John, having completed their tasks before the women, sat in the living room waiting for us. Ray looked up and gazed steadily at me, eyes wide with surprise as I sashayed down the stairs. I wore a pastel yellow, green and beige mid-length dress. A pattern on the front depicted two large giraffes munching on the leaves of a tall tree. It was a simple sleeveless dress made from a delicate voile material. The ensemble was completed with a matching long shirt worn unbuttoned over the dress, and beige pumps. Although bought in Canada, the outfit had an African motif and was appropriate for the day. Ray gushed about the outfit. He'd seen me only in jeans, t-shirt and running shoes since I arrived in Tema; hence his reaction.

The men looked handsome. Ray, dressed in a dark suit and light blue shirt, looked rather urbane. I complimented him in return. Pastor John wore an African-styled suit; yellow pants and a matching loose shirt with rich gold embroidery at the neckline. He also deserved a second glance. Peabody and Marie were dressed in beautifully tailored two-piece skirt suits; Peabody in hunter green and Marie in teal.

Alma had prepared breakfast and as soon as we assembled in the living room she invited us to the dining table for our first meal of the day. Pastor John dashed off the earliest to take care of last-minute preparations at his church. Determined not to be late for Sunday service, Peabody had insisted that Ray order a cab to arrive half an hour before the service commenced, although the Kingdom Hall was only five minutes away. She and Marie were the next to leave. Ray and I walked leisurely out to the main road. He grabbed my hand and held it tightly all the way. Sparks flew up my left arm.

What does this hand-holding mean? Is he just a friendly guy or should I read something into it? Now Yvonne, don't be narrow-minded, the gentleman is a pastor for Christ sake.

Ray flagged a cab driving by and while he sat beside the driver, I reclined in the back. My thoughts reverted to Frieda and the anxiety I'd felt the previous day returned. Today I would finally meet her.

Ray and I walked onto the grounds of the church. He introduced me as a special visitor from Canada to everyone we came across. He succeeded in making me feel special. The muscles of my cheeks tightened significantly from the permanent smile on my face. He led me toward the back of the long one-storey building into a small office, offered me a seat, then rushed out to do his Sunday duties. Shortly after, a woman brought me a cool drink.

Sitting alone in the room on a voluptuous sofa, upholstered in mocha velour, I could hear Pastor John talking to someone in an adjoining room. I sipped my drink and looked around the office. It contained two desks, a filing cabinet and two chairs besides the sofa I was sitting on. Several framed photographs of groups of people hung on the wall, church members no doubt. I got up to take a closer look and noticed that one was a wedding picture of a couple. I peered closer. Pastor John and an attractive woman stared back at me. It was only then that I knew he was married.

Where is his wife? She was certainly not at the townhouse. I will delve into this later.

The office door sprang open and Ray stood there holding the hand of a young girl. I recognized her instantly. The boyish-bob haircut, the large eyes and the slender body were just like her photos. It was Frieda. She wore a pinkish-coloured dress with tinges of gold running through it, a simple straight dress that emphasized her thin figure. I observed two buds that were beginning to protrude. She wore little round earrings, a watch, shoes and socks.

A wide smile covered my face and I extended my arms to her.

"Hello Frieda, how nice to finally meet you."

She stepped bashfully toward me and smiled exposing white teeth in dark gums. "Hello Auntie Yvonne."

I hugged her closely and she stood there awkwardly, not knowing what to do.

Ray broke the ice.

"I'll leave you two to get acquainted. Pastor John will escort you in when service is about to begin." He touched my arm, smiled and left the room, closing the door behind him.

I heard singing coming from the sanctuary, and assumed the choir was practicing.

"Please have a seat here, Frieda." I patted the seat beside me on the sofa and she sat down. I tried everything to coax her to talk but she only answered in one syllables. I gave her a bag of gifts that I'd brought for her.

She took the items out one by one and looked them over.

"Thank you, Auntie," she said.

There was no enthusiasm, no excitement, and no hugs.

Pastor John walked into the room and saved the moment.

"Frieda, you'll get to talk more with Sister Blackwood later; time for you to go to Sunday school."

With that, she stuffed the items back into the shopping bag and left the room. I didn't know what to make of it. Was she just shy, overcome with joy or downright ungrateful?

"Let us enter into the sanctuary, Sister," Pastor John said.

Together we walked into the church. Pastor Ray stood at the entrance and he directed me to a seat in the front row. I preferred to sit in the back and observe, but I wasn't given a choice. Pastor John bounced onto the raised platform and took his seat. The singing I'd heard from the office wasn't the choir; the church didn't have one. It was the congregation led by one of its members. Similar to the Spiritual Baptist, they warmed up the congregation with singing before the pastor preached. This Sunday, attendance was at 50 per cent capacity.

The sanctuary was long and narrow. The walls were painted blue, and blue and white striped drapes hung at the front behind the stage. Grey and beige terrazzo tiles covered the floor. The chairs in the pews had chrome frames with white vinyl seats. Instruments of a small band - an electric keyboard, a guitar and some drums - stood to the left of the stage.

The congregation sang a few more songs; ushers collected the offering, then Pastor Ray read a passage of scripture: Acts chapter 3: 1-11. It articulated the story of the lame man who had always waited outside the *Beautiful Gate* and was eventually healed by Peter. It included the famous verse; "Silver and gold have I none; but such as I have give I thee."

Pastor John stepped up to the podium, welcomed everyone and mentioned that I was in the audience and was a sponsor for one of the students. He asked me to stand and be acknowledged. The congregation applauded. I nodded my thanks and sat down again.

The pastor began to preach using the passage previously read by Pastor Ray as his reference text. As I listened and watched him prowl about the stage like a tiger stalking its prey, I forgot that I was sitting in a lowly church in Ghana. I was transported to a Baptist church in the United States. John assumed the movement and voice intonation of a black American preacher as he spoke and moved about the stage. At the end of many of his sentences, he would shout in a raspy voice, "ARE YOU HEARING, SOMEBODY?"

The congregation responded with "Amen!"

". . . The lameness was not his fault. He walked and leapt and praised God. Why didn't the family put him inside and not outside the *Beautiful Gate* all that time? Everyone has a lame situation. ARE YOU HEARING, SOMEBODY?" He surveyed his audience. Everyone sat at attention. ". . .You're not on this earth to take up space. You're here for a purpose. Don't look down on yourself because you're a woman. . . "

He dived into the subject of women looking for "sugar daddies." Most of the members of the audience were women.

". . . No one can pay for your virginity; no one can pay for your self-esteem. Having a man to provide a home and all that goes with it is not it. You're a whole person. ARE YOU HEARING, SOMEBODY?"

He continued in the same vein and I marvelled that he could link the story of the lame man at the *Beautiful Gate* with the topic of "sugar daddies" and promiscuity, but it seemed to be a subject that irked him and he was obviously trying to get a point across. The audience responded with many amens, and hallelujahs throughout the sermon. I had to admit that John was a powerful preacher. If a woman in the audience had been participating in any such vice or had ideas to do so, I'm convinced she would've repented or changed her mind.

At the end of the service Ray called a cab and he, Frieda and I drove to the townhouse. Pastor John had other things to attend to and promised to join us later that evening.

At the house Frieda and I reclined on the sofa and again I tried to encourage her to open up and speak. She responded with the same one-syllable answers. I changed my tactic and tried open-ended questions but still responses were the bare minimum. Ray had been hanging around and sensed my frustration. He entered the living room and switched on the television. An episode of Mr. Bean was in progress. No one can avoid laughing at Mr. Bean's antics and Frieda was no exception. Soon she and I were howling.

When the program ended she said, "Auntie, I'm tired."

I looked at her droopy eyes and realized she was dying to sleep.

"Would you like to take a nap?"

"Yes, Ma'am."

"Okay, come with me, you can sleep in my bed."

I led her up the stairs and showed her my bed.

"Lie down and get some sleep. When you've rested enough, come back downstairs."

"Thank you." She began to remove her shoes immediately.

I left her, closing the door behind me, and returned to the living room to join Ray.

"Poor girl, no wonder she didn't have much to say; she's dog-tired."

"She probably spent the whole day until late last night at the market," Ray said. "It's hard on a young girl."

I felt much better. She wasn't ungrateful; she was tired.

Pastor John arrived home at 4 p.m. and within minutes of his arrival, Peabody and Marie walked into the house.

"My goodness, you two spent the whole day at church?" I asked.

"No. You know how it is with the sisters and brothers," Peabody said. "Once they hear you are visiting from abroad, everyone wants to take you out. We visited with a couple sisters."

"Well while you were gallivanting, I almost sent out an SOS for you two."

We all laughed at that. It seemed funny then but I had been worried and with good reason. They were two women, strangers to the area, and they knew no one. Besides they had no cell phones to call our hosts if they encountered a problem. Conversely, we had no way of finding them once they left the Kingdom Hall. I consoled myself with the expression from one of Shakespeare's plays, "All's well that ends well." They were now home safely.

Alma announced that supper was ready. I dashed upstairs to fetch Frieda. She was sleeping peacefully. I felt she should've had enough rest and shook her gently.

"Frieda, wake up. Wake up, time for supper."

She opened eyes with dilated pupils and looked at me, then quickly realized where she was.

"Oh Auntie, I was so tired."

"Don't worry about it. Do you feel better now?"

She nodded. "Yes."

"Okay, go to the washroom and splash water on your face then come down for supper; we're waiting."

I left her and joined the others at the dining table. Frieda joined us within a few minutes. Peabody said grace and soon we were eating and talking about the services we had attended. I took pains to mention the wonderful sermon that our host had delivered. He grinned with pride, giving us the full extent of his protruding front teeth.

I felt it was a good time to delve into the matter of the missing wife.

"By the way John, I saw your lovely wedding picture hanging on the wall at your office. Where is your lovely wife?"

He licked his lips twice as all eyes focused on him.

"Oh Mary? She's away."

That answer wasn't good enough for me.

"What do you mean away? Is she out of town visiting someone?"

He looked like a cornered mouse. "I sent her to America to work."

The main vein in Peabody's neck sprang to life at the words "I sent" and she glowered at John.

"You mean she is away living and working in the United States?" she asked.

"Yes. I don't make enough from the church to live on; somebody has to work."

Peabody was ready to say more. I gave her a sharp look. She understood the nonverbal communication and remained silent.

"That's too bad; we would've loved to meet her." In an attempt to change the subject, I said, "John, tell us a bit about your tribe."

He quickly responded. "I'm Efutu. We're from the central region. We're not a large tribe; some people say we're about 150,000."

"What language do you speak, besides English of course?" I asked.
"We speak mainly Guan, but we speak other dialects, too."
I had to ask the burning question about the subject that always bothered me.
"Do your people practice female circumcision?"
"No, we do not."
He obviously had nothing more to say about that subject.
Marie finally waded into the conversation. "You are a Christian; does that mean all Efutus are Christians?"
"Oh no. Some of us are, but many practice the old religions."

After we'd eaten and relaxed, I asked Ray what was on the agenda. He decided to take us down to the harbour. John said he had important paperwork to attend to and passed on the outing. We changed into street clothes and walked out to the main road where Ray hailed a taxi. We dropped off Frieda at her aunt's house on the way to Tema's harbour.
The harbour was large, wide and amazing. We watched huge cranes and heavy equipment loading and unloading all kinds of products. We gathered at a low platform and gazed onto the Atlantic Ocean as dusk began to descend upon Tema. Several ships were docked a little ways out. I counted 14 anchored in the shallow water, waiting their turn to load or unload their cargo. They were all lit up like Christmas trees. The lights from the ships threw a wide shimmering streak across the ocean. Billows rolled, splashed and broke on the shore as white froth ebbed and flowed. Earlier in the day, it had rained briefly, leaving behind remnants of gray skies. I could've stood there and admired the harbour and listened to the crash of the waves all night.
I turned to Ray. "You'd said the harbour was big but I had no idea it was this huge."
"Yes, we're very proud of it. It's one of the largest harbours in West Africa."
"Wow! Very impressive."
After we'd gawked at the harbour for a while, Ray said, "I want to show you the other side." He laughed, obviously knowing something we didn't. "Be warned, it's not as glamorous as this side."
We tore ourselves away from the view and followed Ray to the other side.
What a difference!

It was the place where the fishmongers congregated. Hundreds of women and children waited there. They sat on large enamel basins, like the ones I'd seen women carrying on their heads in Kumasi; they sat on baskets and they sat on buckets, selling their fish. Some were waiting for canoes that hadn't yet returned.

"The men go out and do the fishing and the women do the selling," Ray said.

"But it's so late already," Peabody said.

"Sometimes the men in the canoes don't return until midnight."

"You're kidding," Marie said.

"No. The women have to wait until they come in."

The harbour reeked of rotting fish and other obnoxious odours but the vendors and children seemed oblivious to them. Canoes were scattered all about, some at the water's edge, some pulled up on the sand. Fishing nets were strewn on the sand. It was a marketplace, a bizarre, grim location where time stood still. The women chatted and laughed, accepting their lot without question. Some women had babies in their arms; some had babies on their backs. People just sat around waiting. As dusk deepened, I observed that there was little light, only a covered area with a naked light bulb hanging precariously from the edge. The vendors were basically sitting around in darkness. It was an incredible scene.

The idea of sitting at that harbour, absorbing the elements, inhaling foul odours of rotting fish, waiting around with nothing to do, simply floored me. Why would these women do this week after week, year after year? How profitable could such an occupation be? I imagined the agony and the sorrow they experienced when a husband, brother or son didn't return from the sea – gone forever. I concluded that it must take a special person to work at such an occupation or someone who had lost total perspective on life.

"Life is so tough for some people," Peabody whispered.

I squeezed her hand. I also felt the pain.

SEVENTEEN

ROAD TO TOGO

I HAD NEVER thought of Togo, or even imagined visiting that country, until Akwasi suggested it as an alternative for Mali. My knowledge of Togo was sparse; it was French and was one of two small countries sandwiched between Ghana and Nigeria. That constituted the extent of my knowledge at that time. Peabody and Marie knew even less. But we were adventurous and keen to learn as much about Africa as we could while we were on the continent.

At an appropriate moment after we arrived in Tema, I'd asked Ray to organize a trip for us to visit Togo. He'd agreed and quickly made arrangements for a car and driver. He also volunteered to accompany us. I was thrilled. I wondered if there wasn't pressing church business he had to attend to, but as the saying goes, "Never look a gift horse in the mouth." I thanked him for his offer.

Monday morning after breakfast the taxi arrived. It was the same driver who had driven us from Koby's Hotel. He was a good driver; I felt safe with him. First, we drove to Pastor John's office (He had left earlier to attend to church matters.) where he prayed with us for a safe journey to and from Togo. Then we set out.

Warm air soothed my face as I looked out the open window of the Toyota. The sun climbed steadily in the sky. I knew it would be another hot day. We travelled east and fast, on roads that were in good condition. At noon we stopped at a southern-fried chicken restaurant where we all ate a big lunch; then we continued our journey.

The landscape in the southeast was much different from the Ashanti region. It was Savanna land, flat rolling plains with parched beige grass like dried corn plants in some areas. The vegetation consisted mainly of scrub bushes, interspersed with a few trees. At one point we came upon a large cotton tree that seemed totally out of place. Several cotton bolls were opened, exposing white soft fibre. A mild intermittent wind tickled the tree and cotton fibres floated in the air past our car.

Just ahead of us a truck struggled to negotiate a slight grade. The cab was opened at the back, exposing dozens of white cloth bags the size of pillowcases. I couldn't imagine what the bags contained but the truck was stacked high with them. Suddenly, something moved at the top of the pile. Lying flat on his back, as comfortable as if he were in his bedroom, was a young man. My imagination worked overtime as I watched the lad. What if the truck were to hit a major pothole? I envisaged him flying into the air and landing smack in the middle of the road, only to be run over by another vehicle. I don't think a similar thought ever crossed his mind.

After hours of steady driving, we left the savannas behind and began to pass through several towns. We came to Ada and shortly after, the police pulled us over. It was a checkpoint. Dressed in a navy blue uniform, with a beret on his head, the police officer asked the driver for his documents. He checked them and also peeked inside the trunk. It seemed documents and cargo were both in order because he allowed us to continue without any comments.

Further along the road, several vendors sold bags of charcoal. It was fascinating to observe the different dominant products that vendors marketed in each town. Sometimes it was firewood, sometimes charcoal, other times it was garri or peanuts. The vendors selling garri in Ada packaged it a peculiar way, much differently from the vendors in Kumasi. They wrapped it in a cone-shaped brown paper. In Kumasi, vendors sold garri in transparent plastic bags.

"Ray, can you tell us how they make garri?" I asked.

"Why? You planning to plant cassava?" He looked around and grinned as he teased. We'd developed camaraderie very quickly.

"Why not? I could be the lady farmer of Ghana."

"That would be something." Marie squealed.

After a few more quips Ray supplied the information.

"I know you all know fufu by now. Well, the cassava flour used to make it is garri. First, you dig up the cassava root and peel it, then you wash it. You soak it in water for about two hours, then grate it. You put the grated cassava in a tightly-woven bag that is porous and put some weights on it. The weight helps to squeeze out most of the milky liquid. Sometimes this process takes three days. After that, you spread out what is in the bag to dry in the sun for several hours. When it is dry you sift it and dry roast a little at a time in a big pot over a high fire. Then you have garri."

"And so endeth the lesson," Peabody said. We all laughed.

"Now I understand something I'd noticed the first time I visited Ghana. I saw cassava being dried in the sun along the roadside but I didn't understand why."

"Some folks don't have the space in their homes to do it; that is why."

We came upon an area dotted with anthills near the road. They were various sizes and shapes and made from red clay soil. Peabody and Marie were mesmerized. Although I'd seen this phenomenon before, I still found it difficult to comprehend how tiny ants are able to build such large structures. Some of the anthills stood more than five feet tall.

We arrived at a handsome modern bridge with walkways on either side. A wide, green river flowed lazily below.

"What is the name of the river below?" I asked Ray as we drove along the bridge.

"Is the Volta River."

"No way! I've heard so much about the great Volta Lake and Akosombo Dam. So this is the Volta." I was thrilled, assuming we would soon see the lake.

"Yes, this is it. The Volta is a very long river. You'll cross it a few times."

"How long?" Marie asked.

"It starts up north in Burkina Faso and flows south all the way to the Gulf of Guinea. It's about 1,600 kilometres long. By the way, we're in Eastern Region."

Ghana is divided into 10 regions; Kumasi, where we'd stayed with Afua, was the capital of one region, the Ashanti Region.

After crossing the bridge we came to a town called Sogakope, then a toll booth. Ray paid 500 cedis, the standard price wherever there was a toll. Our driver continued at a good clip, averaging about 120 kilometres an hour. The eastern roads were fairly good except every now and again we would come upon a few bumps and mounds. Whenever we hit a mound we were lifted off the seat.

"If any of us were pregnant we would surely lose the baby." Peabody whispered so that only Marie and I could hear.

Marie somehow found the bouncing amusing; she howled with laughter whenever we hit a mound. Everyone, including the driver, turned to look at her. At Antititi we passed an area that appeared to be swampland. The land was flat and scattered with dozens of little trenches filled with water. The grass was green and thick, not beige and parched as it had been in the savanna areas we'd passed. Ray explained that it was rice paddies.

The town of Affaa was crowded. People scurried along the street. It was lined with stalls and booths. Vendors and buyers moved about selling and buying wares, carrying bundles on their heads, some women with babies on their backs. Life was hectic. Vehicles found it difficult to drive on the main street. Horns blared and tempers flared.

Finally, we arrived at the border of Togo and Ghana. Dozens of money traders sold currency behind small tables at the side of the road. They reminded me of three-card gamblers who were always slight of hand and always won at the guessing-card game. Ray suggested that we purchase some CFA, Togo's currency, there. Under normal circumstances I would be wary about doing any such thing; being a banker made me even more reluctant to do so.

Buy currency at the side of the road from strangers? Is he crazy? How do I know if the money is authentic? And if it is counterfeit, what do I do? To whom do I report it?

But Ray was as serious as a magistrate; he had great faith in the traders.

The driver pulled up at the side of the road and I walked with Ray and my cousins to one of the trading posts. Ray asked the trader for the exchange rate, nodded to us that it was good and we bought our CFAs. No sooner had we bought the currency, it started to rain. The natives began to rush here and there, pushing away anyone and anything in their path; it was like a stampede. To avoid being trampled, we dashed back to the car. Sequestered in the taxi, the five of us watched the rain as it pounded outside. The traffic shuffled along despondently on the wet road while sheets of water, like showers in the movies, slanted passed the windshield. The windows fogged up from our recycled air. The driver cracked his window slightly to allow air to circulate and water sloshed in. At intervals, he wiped the windshield from within, which allowed us to see outside. Everything looked bleak.

"What a way to start our visit to Togo," I said.

"Do you think it will stop raining soon?" Marie asked. She looked uncomfortable. It had gotten warm inside the car and the little air we had was becoming stale.

"These downpours don't usually last long," Ray said.

True to his word, in less than fifteen minutes the rain stopped; the clouds cleared up, and life began to return to normal.

The journey had ended for our driver. He removed our luggage from the trunk and handed them to us. He cleaned all the car windows, bade us goodbye and turned the car around for his return journey to Tema.

Suddenly I felt vulnerable, naked as a new bar of soap. There was no longer a car to hide inside, to shield us from the bustling crowd. Standing at the border of Ghana and Togo, alone with Ray, we were caught up in the mayhem of people pushing and shoving, without a visa to enter Togo. Ray sensed our plight and in his African drawl, spoke reassuringly.

"Don't worry about anything; people always behave like this when it rains. Do you see that narrow track over there?" He pointed to his right.

I looked across the crowd and saw a narrow covered area.

"Yes, I see it," I said.

"Good. We're going to walk under the walkway. Just at the other end are the people who will issue the visas. Hold on to your bags tightly and hold on to each other so you don't get separated. If you get detached, just keep your eyes on me." He looked at each of us and we nodded, indicating that we were ready.

Thank goodness he's six-feet-two and much taller than most of the folks here; he should be easy to spot.

Ray grasped my hand while Peabody and Marie held hands and together the four of us pushed and pressed our way through the crowd until we passed under the walkway. Before we realized it, we were on the other side and on the soil of Togo. A raised platform covered on top, but opened at one side, stood in front of us. I would aptly describe it as a shed. Two men dressed in uniforms sat behind a crude wooden desk. Ray led us toward the platform, and like lambs to the slaughter, we stood before the men.

"Visa!" barked one of the men.

Peabody looked at me. "They can't be serious," she whispered. "This is immigration?"

Ray stepped forward and presented his passport, then explained to the officer that we were tourists from the United States and Canada travelling with him and required visas.

"Let me see yuh passports," the same man said.

We handed him our passports.

"'Ow long yuh stay?"

"About three or four days," Ray answered for us.

"Five thousand fah de Americans and ten thousand fah de Canadian."

"Why is the Canadian more?" I asked.

"I don't know. Dat is de fee fah de visa. Yuh want it or no?" He looked at me with challenge in his eyes.

Geez, no need to be so sanctimonious.

"Of course I want it. I'm just curious."

He provided no further explanation. We paid him the required CFAs. He took his time to flip through each passport. Satisfied with his observations, he stamped them, wrote our names in the blank spaces made by the rubber stamp, and approved seven days for each of us. He then slowly and painstakingly pasted a postage stamp and signed his name in each passport. The other man took even more time to paste the required amount of postage stamps on another document. Peabody and I were dying to laugh but we tried our best to suppress it.

What the heck was this all about? At the rate they're going it will take several hours to process a few visitors.

The downpour earlier had been quick but heavy. It created large muddy puddles in the area; we had to carefully choose where to walk to avoid getting out feet wet. Ray led us towards a taxi stand to select a cab which would take us to Lomé, the capital of Togo. He found a driver that he was satisfied with. My cousins and I huddled together while he negotiated a price for the trip and finally made a deal.

Sitting in the back seat of the taxi heading toward the city, I said to Peabody and Marie, "You know, grandmother used to say that everything happens for a wise purpose. Thank goodness Ray offered to accompany us; it would've been difficult for us to do this on our own."

"Truer words have not been spoken," Peabody said. "He's a life saver."

The taxi driver, Oliver, had a round face and hair cut low to the scalp. His neck was as thick as a baobab stump, his shoulders just as wide. He was a good candidate for a bouncer. He spoke little English, but Ray communicated easily with him in his dialect. He was able to do this because as he'd previously explained, most of the people from Tema, Togo and Benin were from the Ewe tribe; they spoke the same or a similar language.

Oliver took us to Hotel De La Paix. It was a large imposing building, eight stories high, and painted in several shades of blue. Palm trees lined each side of the driveway. Two men sitting behind the reception counter looked at us curiously when we walked into the lobby. It was poorly lit and I didn't see anyone moving about. I inquired about two rooms. Oliver volunteered to speak to them in Ewe and explained who we were. They smiled and one offered apologies in English.

"Sorry ladies, they're renovating the hotel. First time since 40 years."

"Is that so?" I asked. "They haven't done any renovations in 40 years?"

"Yes Madame. We're really not taking any guests as the rooms are dusty and there's no food service."

"Oh that's too bad. Is there another hotel nearby?"

The other man chipped in. "They could maybe use one of the cottages; they're okay."

"Yes, yes, you're right," said the first man. "I forgot about them."

"Why don't you take us to have a look and then we can decide," I said. If the hotel was undergoing massive renovations I didn't want to be on a worksite.

"Okay, Pierre, you take them to see the one near the front," the first man said.

Pierre escorted us to the cottage. It was a cute apartment with oval windows that looked like giant portholes. A large sea-grape tree grew in front of the building, its branches and thick leaves providing shade and privacy for the cottage. At the right was a small flower garden with pretty red flowers. The cottage had two large bedrooms and two bathrooms. A cozy living and dining room separated the bedrooms. It was clean and in order for guests. We returned with Pierre to the main building and advised the receptionist that we would take the cottage. He offered us a discount because everything was not as it should be; no restaurant service for one.

Oliver helped Ray to take our luggage into the cottage. Once inside I pulled Ray aside.

"Oliver seems like a nice driver," I said. "Do you think we should book him to take us around while we're here?"

"Yes, that's a good idea. I was talking with him while you were making arrangements with the receptionist and he says he's from this area and knows the country very well."

"Great, let's use him."

I paid Oliver then popped the question.

"Oliver, how would you like to take us around while we're in Togo?"

"Oui Madame. Where yuh want to go?"

"We don't really know. We just want to see a good cross-section of the county. Take us through the city, any natural tourist attractions, that sort of thing."

Ray explained in Ewe what I'd said.

"No problem. I take you all over."

Togo is a long narrow country, 600 kilometres north to south. It is one of the smallest countries in West Africa and, at that time, had a population of almost four million people.

"By the way Oliver, since we are so close to Benin, I wouldn't mind going to the border."

"Oui Madame."

"Can you pick us up here and take us to another hotel for breakfast tomorrow? Say 9 o'clock?"

"Oui Madame, 9 in de morning."

Ray and Oliver exchanged a few words; then Oliver departed.

Oliver may have been African, Togolese to be precise, but he certainly behaved like a West Indian. He arrived at 10 for the 9 o'clock appointment we'd scheduled. He wore a navy blue and yellow Hawaiian shirt and a pair of peach slacks, confirming my belief that unlike Caribbean men, African men are not shy to wear colourful clothes. We were annoyed with his tardiness. But what do you do in a situation such as this? Should we tell him to take a hike? We needed a reliable, safe driver to take us around and we knew of no other. He did apologize for his tardiness, however, and that was a good sign. Peabody and I bit our tongues, accepted the apology and asked him to take us to a nice hotel for brunch. Breakfast time had elapsed; now the meal would be brunch as far as I was concerned.

Oliver drove through the town of Lomé, situated at the southern most tip of the country, on the coast where it jutted into the Atlantic

Ocean. It was a fairly modern town with many stores and boutiques. We entered the gates of an imposing building. A unique structure, it was designed like a huge boat propped up on elongated triangular columns. Painted in pale delicate pink, the hotel had a banner of *bas relief* that ran along the front wall. Oliver parked in front, away from the walkway and we entered a spacious inviting lobby. The Sarakawa Mercure Hotel with its 164 rooms, many with balconies, was impressive. Oliver obviously knew his way around and led us through the lobby onto a pathway, past an Olympic-size swimming pool, its turquoise water inviting us to jump in, to a large restaurant with buffet-style dining. The Sika-Sika dining room was airy and nestled among palm tress. The sides were open, giving us a view of tourists romping in the pool and the ocean between the trees. Dozens of bright blue lounge chairs and beach umbrellas were arranged around the pool. We sat at a table in the middle of the room where we could see the guests' comings and goings. Most of them were white. The gentle lapping of the waves of the Atlantic Ocean was ever present.

We were enjoying a delicious brunch, chatting and laughing while trying to get to know Oliver and Ray better, when two lizards pranced onto the floor. They seemed to be sparing with each other. Marie and I jumped to our feet and shrieked as if we were being attacked by a giant reptile. A waiter rushed to our aid and when we showed him the object of our freight, he grinned and shooed the critters away.

"You don't have to worry about the lizards Miss; they're tame."

"Thanks, but it has nothing to do with being tame," I said. "I just don't like them near me."

After that, the waiter kept a keen look out for lizards. A few more appeared, but he chased them away before they came close to us. I didn't enjoy our 34,000 CFA brunch much after the incident.

EIGHTEEN

TOGO'S AFRICA GIN

OLIVER SOON gathered that we wanted to see a good cross-section of his country, thanks to a little coaxing from Ray. First, he offered to take us to see a waterfall. Waterfalls are always great tourist attractions. In my homeland, Jamaica, a tourist hasn't seen the island until she's seen and climbed Dunn's River Falls. In Ontario, my home for more than thirty years, Niagara Falls is one of our greatest attractions, indeed, one of the greatest wonders of the modern world. Now filled with excitement and anticipation, I was on my way to see one of nature's most intricate phenomena, a waterfall in Togo.

For awhile, the road led us past a scenic indented coastline with white sand beaches; then it spiralled north, leaving the city behind us. There was a marked difference in the appearance of the houses, farms, and the landscape from those in Ghana. Togo seemed more organized, more careful about outward appearances. Fences weren't made from rusted, dilapidated galvanized zinc; instead the natives plaited palm leaves and made attractive modest fences around their homes.

A spectacular narrow country, Togo is a mosaic of towns, villages and farms. At that time of the year the vegetation was lush. Over steep hills and down grassy valleys, Oliver drove carefully while chatting non-stop in dialect to Ray. It seemed as if the two men had known each other all their lives. In the small towns, similar to Ghana, people dressed in multi-coloured clothing lined the streets to sell their wares. I found it interesting that although Ghana and Togo were neighbours, and many of the inhabitants were from the same Ewe tribe, their ways of doing things were different in many respects.

Oliver took us to an indoor market. Stalls were stocked full of many types of fresh fruits and vegetables organized like a work of art. I felt guilty removing items for fear of disturbing the design. In Ghana the markets were slipshod, piled high with yams and cassava and few vegetables. The difference was conspicuous and I wondered why. After sometime I figured it out; Togo was French. The colonial masters from France had brought their particular brand of culture to the natives; it reflected in their food, clothes and even the way they took care of their farms.

As we traversed the countryside, the men shared jokes and stories with my cousins and me. Ray told us a fascinating anecdote: some four hundred years ago a king ruled his ancestors, the Ewes. At that time the people lived in a city surrounded by a thick, high wall. The king was brutal and treated his subjects badly, but they had no means of escape. Then one day someone had an idea. He shared it with his neighbours. Whenever the villagers washed clothes or had to dispose of water, they began to throw it on a certain spot on the wall. After a period of time the area softened and weakened. One night when the king and his guards were asleep the citizens escaped by breaking through the wall. They walked backwards so that the king's guards couldn't track their footprints. Ray proclaimed ardently that the story was true.

I'd heard several stories about palm wine on my first journey to West Africa but never had the occasion to taste it. It has been said that: it is an aphrodisiac; the Ashanti Kings drank it; women shouldn't drink it. The mystery of the drink only heightened by determination to try it before I returned to Canada. In Togo, the opportunity presented itself.

We were cruising along the countryside, passing through Kebe, when we came upon a stall with a crude cardboard sign that read *Palm Wine.*

"Stop the car Oliver; I want to get some of that stuff," I said from the back seat.

Ray looked around at me as if I'd grown horns.

"You want palm wine?" he asked, his inference clear; I must be crazy.

"Sure, anything wrong with that?"

Being the gentleman that he is, he didn't oppose me openly.

"I don't know. It's just an unusual request, I guess."

"Well I've been hearing about it for so long I want to see what it's all about."

It was a good time to stretch our legs anyway. We all piled out of the car and walked over to the small makeshift stall manned by a lad of about fourteen. He had several plastic bottles of the smokey-coloured liquid on display. Ray took charge and spoke to the lad.

Turning to Marie, I said, "Hey, you want to try it?"

"Sure, I wouldn't mind tasting it."

"I'm not drinking any of that stuff," Peabody said.

"Its alcoholic anyway, so you shouldn't have it."

Before I could place my order the vendor ran toward the bushes.

"What happened Ray?" I asked. "Where's he going? What did you say to him?"

"You should always drink palm wine when it's fresh; the older it gets, the more potent it is. He's gone to get fresh bottles."

Whatever gave him the idea that I wouldn't want the potent stuff? That's what I want!

The lad soon returned with three more bottles of palm wine. I bought a bottle of the new stock. The predicament was, Marie and I wanted to have some immediately, but we had no cups and the bottle was clumsy to drink from. The lad offered us calabashes. I used my bottled water to rinse them (I always carried bottled water in my purse.) then poured a good slug of the wine in each. Marie and I tasted the precious liquid for the first time.

"How's it?" Ray asked, looking anxiously at Marie and me.

"It's not at all what I expected." I said. "It has a very quaint taste, nothing like wine."

"I don't really like it." Marie scrunched up her face.

"Well at least you tried it. I'll take the rest home."

Peabody, having no interest in palm wine or any alcohol for that matter, had wandered off while we sampled the mystery drink. She suddenly called out to me,

"Yvonne, look! Jackfruit!"

Across the street from the palm wine vendor was a large jackfruit tree laden with fruits at different stages of development.

"Jackfruit indeed! I haven't seen any in Ghana so far. Let's take some photos."

I handed Ray my camera and asked him to take pictures of us. We crossed the road and posed beside the jackfruit tree. Large green fruits with soft spiky protrusions grew mainly from the trunk of the tree instead of from the branches. We were able to touch the fruits as we posed. While Ray prepared to take the shot, Marie, who rarely says anything, decided to be poetic.

"Mother, daughter and cousin,
Underneath the jackfruit tree.
Across the street in hot sun,
Is African palm wine, not rum!"

She howled with laughter and the rest of us joined in.

As we continued our tour of Togo we began to see some similarities to Ghana.

Furniture such as beds, settees, and chairs were being sold at the side of the road. In the same manner, we saw coffins being sold. An ornate one, painted in white with gold trim all around was proudly displayed.

Similar to Ghana, students wore uniforms, but Togo had different colour schemes; boys wore khaki pants with white shirts, girls wore khaki tunics with white or light blue blouses. Mothers carried their babies in slings on their backs.

I spotted an ackee tree covered with fruits and wondered if the Togolese people ate them. A few years earlier, while visiting Nigeria, I'd seen ackee trees there but my sister-in-law had mentioned that Nigerians didn't eat the fruit. For me, there's nothing quite like a breakfast with ackee and codfish. Ackee with codfish is Jamaica's national dish.

We passed through more small towns and I observed other differences. On the street, vendors sold unwrapped breads, but unlike the plump, golden brown breads in Ghana, these were slender, crusty baguettes (just like you would see in France). In Togo mopeds or scooters were a popular mode of transportation; I saw them everywhere.

At the town called Akepe, a young man stood at the side of the road holding a snake with dark skin punctuated with yellow spots. This beautiful creature was about two metres long. Inside the car we jumped up and down and screeched. Peabody covered her eyes, not wanting to see any reptiles. I suspected that at that moment she wished she was far away from Africa.

A thick patch of tall trees with distinctive gray bark came into view. I'd seen many of these trees in Ghana and had inquired about the name but no one seemed to know. Oliver came to the rescue and solved the puzzle by providing the answer; it was teak.

We'd travelled a couple of hours when Oliver swung the car off the main road and unto a narrow unpaved track. We drove a short distance and came upon a small clearing in the bushes. A low hut with a thatch roof was partially hidden in a secluded corner. A slender palm tree, about 10 metres tall, towered above the hut. It was a species I'd never seen before. A cluster of several small red-brown nuts hung like a bunch of grapes from the top of the tree. Oliver parked the car and stepped out. My cousins and I exchanged fearful glances.

What the heck is he doing taking us into the bushes?

Before we could question him, Oliver said, "I want yuh to see how deh mek *Africa Gin.*"

"Africa Gin? Do you know anything about this, Ray?" I asked.

"Oh yeah, they make it in the bush in Ghana, too."

"What is it really?" Peabody wanted to know.

"It's a kind of bootleg liquor. They make it from palm wine."

Oliver plodded in the direction of the hut with the rest of us trailing behind. We arrived in the thick of things; production was well underway. Three men, all under 25, were the bootleggers. They were working outdoors, a short distance from the hut. Oliver explained that the hut was their residence while they made the Africa Gin, but they lived elsewhere. Oliver greeted the men and rattled off something in dialect. They argued back and forth. I assumed he was assuring them that we weren't spies. After the discussion, the men agreed to show us the procedure.

A yellow plastic bucket filled with fresh palm wine stood on the ground. A large tin container, covered with soot, was perched over a roaring fire nearby. The content was boiling and gurgling. One of the men stoked the fire and added more wood. The first man dipped a round gourd into the yellow bucket, filled it with palm wine and dumped it into the big container that stood over the fire. Attached to this container were metal pipes. The pipes were attached at their other end to three more tin cans. These cans were uncovered and brown from rust. Oliver explained that when the palm wine boiled to a certain temperature, it gave off steam; the steam was trapped and transported through the pipes to the other containers. After condensation this became Africa Gin and was bottled and sold. A large glass jar stood on the ground, filled with a clear liquid – bootleg Africa Gin!

"So what is the alcoholic content of this 'gin'?" I asked. The bootleggers stared at me, but refused to respond. "Does anyone know? Does anyone care?" I stared back at them.

"It's about 70 per cent alcohol," Ray said.

"Wow! Can I taste it?"

I'd been excited about tasting palm wine, but to taste Africa Gin would be something else! Looking around at the process and containers, I concluded that it was not sanitary, but it was alcohol so I didn't think it would hasten my death. I held out my right hand, curving it like a cup. One of the bootleggers held up a jar and poured some in my palm. I tasted the liquid. Instantly, my mouth exploded on fire. It felt as if I'd swallowed a mouthful of cognac.

"People should have a prescription to drink this stuff," I said, barely able to speak. I quickly gulped a mouthful of water from my water bottle. "I think it is much higher than 70 per cent alcohol."

We left the Africa Gin makers and came upon a mountain range that stretched across the country. It was mainly undulating hills. Oliver said it was Pitacue but he was unable to spell it for us. I learned later that it was the Ouatchi Plateau and that the highest peak was Pic d'Agou. I guess that is what Oliver was trying to say. We continued on narrow roads that meandered through verdant forest as we ascended another hill. Tall trees formed an arch across the road, which allowed the bright sunlight to penetrate the canopy only intermittently. Our car laboured up the hill and finally, Oliver pulled up at the side of the road. He turned to us in the back seat.

"We will walk from here to de waterfall, okay?"

Well of course it is okay. It is obvious that we can't drive up to it.

We stepped out of the car and Oliver collected two stones from the side of the hill and placed one up against each back tire. We followed our guide a short distance down the hill we'd just ascended. The atmosphere under the canopy of trees was tranquil, the scene breathtaking. I looked over the side of the road and shivered. A deep, dark precipice loomed up at me. Traffic was noticeably absent on the stretch of road at that time. All was quiet except for the occasional chirping of birds. It felt as if we were lost in a forest.

Without warning the tranquility was shattered by the sound of the splash and gurgle of water. The waterfall was close by. Just slightly off the road, partially hidden in the bushes, was the skinniest, most delightful waterfall I'd ever seen. Crystal clear water tumbled off boulders, falling downhill several metres. It cascaded over rocks and flora to be finally deposited in an Eden-like pool with water lilies and other flowering water-grown plants, blanketed with pink, purple and white blooms. As the water hit the pool it splashed on us and created ripples. All the way from top to bottom, the waterfall was less than a metre wide. My cousins and I stood at the edge of the pool admiring and enjoying the view, the distinct babble of the water, the smell of moist earth, the flowering plants and the thick emerald vegetation. I would be remiss if I didn't say I was disappointed by the size of the waterfall; it was certainly no Niagara Falls. But after the initial surprise, I truly enjoyed the ambience and atmosphere. We tarried there for a while and took pictures.

Back up the steep hill we trekked with Oliver leading the way. Ray held my hand and practically dragged me up the slope. We were about to enter the car when Oliver advised us to wait. He had to turn it around first. A nail-biting moment ensued as we watched him maneuver the automobile while trying to avoid driving off the road and onto the precipice below. He reversed, drove forward, turned, and locked the steering several times before he had the car facing the downhill direction and ready for the descent. Only then did we breathe once more and join him in the car.

We descended the mountain without incident. Oliver drove carefully and slowly until the road levelled off. Soon the landscape became dotted with farms and small towns once more. Occasionally we came upon small cemeteries, usually with 10 or 12 tombs, along the side of the road. One of these cemeteries had an elaborate tomb and Oliver slowed down to a crawl, allowing us to scrutinize it. The tomb was wide, thick and covered in glossy black and white tiles arranged like a checkerboard. The head stone, made from marble, had raised lettering with the deceased information.

"Mmm, that must be King Tut!" Peabody nudged me with her elbow.

Ray overheard her and responded.

"Sometimes they spend everything they have on funerals here. It's important to have a good burial."

"That's amazing," I said. "With all the poverty around, you would think emphasis would be placed on the living and not the dead." I thought about Afua's brother and the long mourning period with all the activities that took place prior to interment; it seemed the cost of that burial would mount into millions of cedis. But traditions die hard in Africa.

On the way back to Lomé, a man sped by on a scooter with a woman passenger at his back. She carried a large basket of fruits on her head. She held the basket with one hand and with the other she gripped the driver around the waist.

Peabody winked at me. "Only in Togo, eh?"

NINETEEN

THE DRIVER FROM HELL

LATER THAT evening, Oliver drove us to a restaurant for dinner. A grin spreads across my face every time I recall dinner at the restaurant. We were escorted to a table overlooking the street. It was an average restaurant, nothing fancy. We had anticipated sampling the local Togolese cuisine. We reviewed the menu and my cousins and I ordered a dish with chicken, one of the few items we recognized. Ray and Oliver both ordered the same dish – pork. When the waiter brought their meal, my eyes almost popped out of my head. He delivered two chunky legs of roasted pork served on thick pieces of wood, like butcher blocks, to the table! French fries, enough to feed a Boy Scout troop, were served with them. He placed steak knives that looked like small machetes beside the blocks. Visions of Fred Flintstones holding a large leg of meat by the bone in the centre and ripping it with his bare hands came to my mind. I was too curious to let the opportunity slip by; I asked Ray if I could taste his. He obliged readily by chopping off a piece of the meat and feeding me with it. It was tender and tasted very good – like smoked ham. The size of the serving blew me away. I watched subtly to see if Ray and Oliver would be able to eat it all. They did.

The next day Oliver took us on a tour of markets and the eastern side of the country. Once I'd learned that Benin, the adjoining country to the east, was easy to access by car, I wanted to visit it also. From the back seat of the car, I tapped Ray on the shoulder.

"It would be a pity to come this far and not at least set foot on Benin. Can you ask Oliver how long it would take us to drive to the border?"

"But you don't have any visa for that country; you won't be able to get in without one."

"I know. I don't want to spend money on a visa since we don't plan to spend time there; I just want us to step in, step out, just to say we touched the soil of Benin."

Ray looked at me with an expression that said, "You are strange," but he acquiesced to my wishes and spoke to Oliver in Ewe.

"Oliver says it will take half an hour."

"You're kidding. Are you sure? I can't believe Togo is so narrow that we can get to another country in such a short time."

"It sounds kinda short to me too; we'll see," Ray said.

We came upon a wide murky river.

"Dat is de Togo River," Oliver said.

There were several small canoes on the river.

"What are they doing in those canoes?" Marie asked.

"Oh dose? Dey call dem Pirogues. Dey tek people and cargo across to de odda side."

"Like a ferry?"

"Oui. Yuh want to try it?"

"No way!" Marie said. "It doesn't look that safe to me."

The Pirogues were long and narrow, and loaded with people and cargo. Similar to gondolas in Venice, a man with a long pole stood near the end of each one and guided it along the path.

"If it overturns you just swim to shore." Ray said.

"I can't swim."

"Okay, I just keep driving," Oliver said and let go a loud laugh.

While ferrying across the river would've been faster, we drove along a circuitous road until we reached the other side. Oliver stopped at a restaurant overlooking the river at Agbodrafor. We sat and admired the view and watched the river activities from a wide patio at the side of the restaurant. We sipped cool drinks while the sun blazed down on us. Some of the canoes were so laden with cargo that we wondered if a miracle had saved them from capsizing. The men in charge were obviously skilled; they kept the boats afloat.

Peabody gazed at the river in awe. "The Togo River is quite wide and long."

"Yes, it goes right into Benin," Oliver said, alternating between

French and English.

"Do they catch fish in it?" Marie asked

"Yes, yes, dey catch tilapia and odda fish."

We tarried at the restaurant for a while; then began our journey toward Benin. The landscape was picturesque with snippets of ocean view appearing every now and again. Along the way we passed vendors selling various products, but I found a most interesting one I'd never seen being sold along the road before – gasoline. Many vendors in stalls along the way sold four and eight litre bottles of gasoline. I don't recall any gas stations along the road we travelled, and concluded that the vendors were providing a valuable service. Then I thought of the product. How could you be sure it wasn't watered down? Would it hurt or help your automobile? I thought of the CFAs we'd bought on the side of the road. As with many things in Africa, you had to have an abundance of faith.

At exactly four hours after we'd set out on our journey we arrived at the border of Togo and Benin. I thought back to the conversation I'd had with Ray. "Oliver says it will take half an hour." Some half an hour! Maybe something got lost in the translation.

At the confluence where the Togo River meets the Atlantic Ocean, I gazed, riveted. Oliver pulled over to the side of the road and we walked over to watch as the murky, freshwater river was absorbed into the cobalt blue, salty Atlantic Ocean. It was like mixing a huge never-ending cocktail. From one direction waves splashed over a cluster of boulders which formed a natural barrier across the meeting place of ocean and river. The waves receded and regrouped while the calm docile river flowed lazily into the waves and its colour changed in a blink. The water was obviously shallow in the area and little children frolicked in it, playing tag with the waves. Small mounds of red silt formed islands in the area and birds swooped down to snatch fish they'd spotted from above.

Within minutes after leaving the scenic estuary we arrived at the border where the people of Togo and Benin crossed into each other's country. Border-crossing personnel talked with people attempting to cross.

"Ray, would you tell Oliver to ask the guard if we could cross over for five minutes?" I asked.

Ray looked at me with wide-eyed surprise.

"You really want to go over to Benin?"

"Yeah, for a few minutes, just to say we were in Benin."

The look on Ray's face told me he doubted it could be done, but he relayed the message to Oliver.

"Yuh want to go over dere?" he asked.

"Yes. Just ask please. It's either yes or no." The men were beginning to annoy me. What did we have to lose?

Oliver spoke to the border guard and pointed at us. Maybe it was our honest- looking faces, I'm not sure what it was, but the guard agreed without hesitation.

"We don't do dis. . . but yuh can come over. . .10 minutes, okay? " he said in halting English. "Yuh go just to dat place over dere, okay?"

He pointed to a row of stalls where the natives sold local crafts.

We thanked him and promptly crossed the border into Benin. We strolled around the small stalls and admired the items. As we had no Benin currency, we couldn't purchase anything. When the time allotted expired, we returned to the guard. He allowed us back into Togo with a wave and a smile.

The next day Oliver took us to the Togo/Ghana border. He had been a helpful, pleasant man. We thanked him profusely and tipped him well when we bade him goodbye. The task at hand was for Ray to select a driver to take us on the long drive back to Ghana. Dozens of taxis lined up on both sides of each country, waiting for passengers, especially ones that looked like tourists. The drivers spotted us the moment we crossed into Ghana and several tried to solicit our business. Ray stood his ground, protected us from the mob and did all the talking. He wanted a responsible driver with a car in good condition and the price had to be reasonable. After arguing back and forth with two drivers, he finally selected a driver with a black Subaru. The car was clean and seemed to be in good order. The driver was a five-foot-two, middle-aged man, dressed neatly with his shirt tucked into tailored slacks. He wore sunglasses. Maybe that should have given us a hint. He greeted us warmly, placed our luggage in the trunk of his car and we piled in, with Ray taking the front seat.

The driver started out at a good clip and we began to relax as our comfort level increased. We crossed a long, wide bridge over the Volta River and again admired the river. At 5:45 p.m. we arrived at Attoape. The sun disappeared behind a thick, moving dark cloud. I could barely see sprays of light indicating that it was still around somewhere. By 6 o'clock it was dark and the sun had totally disappeared. Now the driver began to exhibit his true colours. He drove in the middle of the road. At times we were mere inches away from the oncoming traffic. Peabody, Marie and I gripped the seat, then each other. We sighed and we began to pray. He still wore his dark glasses. I asked him if he could see. I suppose he got the hint because he removed the glasses and placed them atop his head.

We continued our journey and although it was dark, the oncoming cars drove at full speed without headlights. The roads had no streetlights. We were scared to death. Within an hour we were pulled over at yet another checkpoint, the fifth since the journey began. I was happy for the break. At each checkpoint, an officer opened the trunk and checked inside.

We arrived back in Tema in a much shorter time than it had taken us to get to Togo. Thanks to the driver, we were nervous wrecks. Peabody paid him with a small tip. Back at the townhouse we prayed and expressed gratitude for a safe delivery.

TWENTY

LOGBA TOTA

When John Denver sang about *Almost Heaven, West Virginia,* he obviously hadn't visited Ghana, but more specifically, Logba Tota. If he had, another song would have been spawned – *Almost Heaven, Logba Tota.*

Ray and I were sitting alone in the living room later in the night after we'd returned from Togo. He had changed into a pair of shorts and a large loose African shirt that ballooned around his slim figure. He looked boyish and cute. He sat on the rug close to where I was sprawled out on the sofa. Peabody was taking a shower while Marie, totally exhausted, had flopped into bed almost immediately after we entered the house.

Ray rested his head on my lap and lightly touched my hand. "Yvonne, I want to take you up into the mountains, into the Volta Region to an area of Hohoe District. There's a place there called Logba Tota," he said in his quiet African drawl. "It's beautiful; you'll enjoy it. We have a sub-church there. One of Pastor John's friends has a cottage up there but he lives in Tema, so he usually allows us to use it. We'll spend a night there."

I hadn't yet recovered from our return trip from Togo with the driver from hell. I was still sore from all the bumps we'd hit in the road. But a trip into the blue-green mountains appealed to me greatly. When would I have this opportunity again? Within a day or two, I would be leaving Tema and saying goodbye to Ray, Frieda and Pastor John. I didn't want to miss a single thing.

"I would love to go. That is so thoughtful of you Ray." The name of the place sounded vaguely familiar. I tapped into my memory bank and contents of an e-mail flooded my mind. "I've heard of that place."

"You have?" Ray pulled away. He looked shocked, as if I'd spoiled his surprise.

"Yes, I remember now. I don't know all that much about it but Anita Sinclair mentioned it in one of her e-mails. I recall she described it as, 'peaceful and tranquil, like heaven.' "

"Well, you'll get to see for yourself." Ray recovered and beamed up at me. "I have a special place up there where I like to just sit and dream."

"Your little secret hiding place, eh?"

His eyes locked onto mine and we laughed, each thinking our own thoughts about the place. I noticed he hadn't included Peabody and Marie in the offer. For a brief moment I envisaged the two of us alone, up in the mountains, then realizing it would be too romantic, too tempting, I said, "I know Peabody and Marie will enjoy it, we'll all go."

If he had any romantic notions there wasn't much he could say that wouldn't expose his hand. He nodded in agreement.

I liked Ray from the moment we met. He seemed so unpretentious, so pure. He liked to hold my hand at every opportunity, just a casual handholding that I never quite understood. Although he had a totally different personality, somehow he reminded me of Adamson. There was no denying that a certain chemistry had developed between the two of us.

What is it about these tall, young Africans that seemed to have an effect on me? I must give my head a shake.

I decided to probe into his personal life, to find out a bit more about him.

"Ray, I know you're single, but do you not have a serious girlfriend?"

"No, I don't have a serious girlfriend."

Okay, that was cut and dried.

"I'm sure you must have had one at sometime. What happened?"

He gazed at me steadily, and as he thought about it, a morass of pain crept across his face. When he spoke, his voice was even and controlled.

"All right, I did have a steady girlfriend, but we broke up."

"Sorry to hear. I noticed a few attractive ladies in the church last Sunday. You have no interest in any of them? Are you not interested in marriage?"

"After the breakup I made up my mind that I'm not dating or marrying anyone unless she is a western woman."

By western he meant a foreigner.

"So how do you plan to meet this 'Western' woman since you live and work in this remote part of Ghana?"

"Well for one thing, we always have people from the U.S.A. coming here on missionary trips. I've met a few nice ladies that way."

I thought of Pastor John's sermon the previous Sunday about women looking for sugar daddies. Maybe Ray found his local Ghanaian women too demanding and felt a foreigner would be more of a giver than a taker.

"It sounds like a tall order Ray, but I wish you well on that score."

He patted my hand. "Thanks, I know I'll find someone."

The next day was designated the day for the trip to Logba Tota. Ray contacted Joe, one of his regular taxi drivers, to take us on the journey. Peabody and Marie had perked up after a good night's rest and were ready to embark on another adventure. Before we departed, Alma, the maid, prepared a delicious lunch of chicken and vegetable soup with sweet potatoes and yams. Pastor John said grace before we ate and he also prayed for us to have a safe journey to and from Logba Tota. We gobbled down the meal; then my cousins and I packed our overnight bags.

The journey began as an interesting one. We travelled east, the way we'd gone when we visited Togo, but soon we headed north to an area where we'd never been before. As the car sped along and the city of Tema began to disappear, the landscape changed. We drove through several small towns, each with its own distinctive make up. At Kpong, dramatic mountains with the most enchanting shapes emerged in the distance. To our right a clutter of huge boulders jutted out from the mountainside. One resembled an elephant; another appeared like a soldier wearing a cap on his head. Just outside of Atimposma we came upon a large bridge with an attractive overhead arch. We watched a calm river flowing lethargically beneath. It was the mighty Volta River again; it seemed we couldn't escape it.

The Volta River is Ghana's most important drainage system. I recalled that Ray had said it stretches 1,600 kilometres (a thousand miles) from Tamale in the north to its mouth at Ada east of Accra. It draws its water from many tributaries and includes the Black Volta and the White Volta.

The trees in Africa were fascinating. Not all looked like the acacia. Most had interesting shapes, and were always capped with luxuriant foliage, but the natives barely noticed them and no one seemed to know any of the names. The name of the huge majestic trees with crusty grey trunks and thick foliage seen all over the country remained a mystery. Through research, I discovered it was called the baobab tree.

At Kpundu, we stopped to purchase oranges from a street vendor, one of several ladies sitting side by side along the road selling fruits. Four cost one thousand cedis.

Peabody was vocal as she'd been many times during our tours.

"They all sell the same things," she said. "How much money can they make selling the same stuff? They have no imagination."

I also wondered at the wisdom of the vendors; there seemed to be more sellers than buyers. But they sat at the side of the road and waited. The women of Ghana seem to spend an inordinate amount of time waiting. They waited in markets for buyers. They waited at the harbour for fishermen. They waited at the side of roads for sales. Their lives seemed to be a never-ending wait.

Two hours later we were on the final leg of the journey. But Ray hadn't divulged an important bit of information. The final stretch of road to our destination was brutal.

Joe had an average-sized car, a Toyota painted in dark blue with yellow strips along the sides. We had driven with him twice before and felt that the car was in good condition. When he turned off the main road onto a narrow dirt road, we had no concerns.

We admired the vegetation. It was more luxuriant than we'd seen anywhere else. Ray explained that it was rain forest country. Cocoa trees were abundant with fruits. Bamboo plants grew in profusion clustered together. The grass grew tall, tender green and succulent. The road turned steeper and steeper and the engine began to labour. We passed folks walking along the road; they carried large bundles on their heads. When they heard the car approaching, they hurried off the road onto the grass.

The road was strewn with many potholes, but it seemed that Joe couldn't spot them early enough because he drove into them. Peabody and I cringed whenever we hit one. From our backseat position, we could hear every scrape, squeak and scratch that was inflicted upon Joe's muffler and undercarriage. The grinding sound of metal on rocks, metal on anything else on the road, resounded in our ears. We came upon two narrow bridges at short intervals from each other. It took some degree of maneuvering before we could get across. On both occasions, convinced that the undercarriage of the taxi would be ripped off, my cousins and I volunteered to get out of the car so that Joe could make the grade and keep his car intact. He thanked us but said it wasn't necessary. The road was a single lane track that could only facilitate one car at a time. We prayed that there would be no other vehicles travelling from the opposite direction. The good Lord answered our prayers.

Peabody, usually talkative and jovial, became very quiet during the manoeuvrings. I turned to look at her and became concerned. She was obviously experiencing stress and tension. I knew that wasn't good for a diabetic. She was probably chiding herself for coming on the trip. Marie said nothing except the occasional "Oh, oh," when blows to the undercarriage were brutal. I thought about Joe. Was the payment Ray had negotiated with him enough to put his car through such vile punishment? Was he regretting taking the assignment? If he did, he never let on.

The sun, a large orange ball, had shone brightly all the way; now it glided over the trees as we travelled north. At 5:30 p.m. as if on cue, it disappeared into the western skies. Before we knew it, darkness enveloped the area. We had arrived in Logba Tota.

Poised at the pinnacle of a steep hill, almost at a 90-degree angle, stood the house where we would spend the night. In a heroic attempt, Joe gunned the motor to ascend the hill. Suddenly, the engine died. We quickly scrambled out of the car and Ray and Joe unloaded our belongings and brought them to the front porch of the house where the caretaker greeted us. Afterwards the two men returned to the vehicle to try to get it started again. It took several tries with both men pushing and rocking the car before Joe was able to drive it up the hill. He parked it in front of the house. I knew that unlike the ascension, he would have no problem descending the hill when we had to leave.

We entered the house and surveyed the facility. There were three average-sized, furnished bedrooms, a large kitchen, a four-piece bathroom and a spacious living room with a colour TV. The floors were covered with glossy ceramic tiles. The windows and front door were protected with decorative wrought-iron grills.

"Hey Ray, your friend has a nice house here." My voice was filled with surprise. Ray had said that we would stay in a friend's cottage; I was therefore expecting accommodation of a lesser calibre.

"Yeah, you know how these guys are; they come back to their village and build big houses but they don't live in them. It's just for show. Whenever there's a funeral or celebration in the village he allows the people to use it."

"This kind of thing seems to be cultural," I said. "I remember a girlfriend who married an Ibo from Nigeria doing a similar thing. For many years they spent a lot of their earnings on building a house in his village while all the time they lived in the city in houses provided by the companies that they worked for. They completed the house about ten years later. When she showed me pictures of it I couldn't believe my eyes. It was a mansion! A huge white mansion. The ironic thing about it is, it's a white elephant. They have no immediate plans to live in that house, maybe when they are old and gray. Their children were all educated in the United States and if they return to Nigeria, they certainly wouldn't be living in the village. I've always pondered on what was the rationale behind building such a house in the village, surrounded by decrepit shacks."

"Just for show, Yvonne, just for show," Ray said.

After sorting out our sleeping arrangements we had a light supper and tried to unwind by watching TV. I had observed a satellite dish in the yard to the right side of the house as we arrived. It provided several channels for us to choose from. But we were all exhausted. We retired to bed early that night.

The next morning I awoke to the sound of roosters crowing. I'd planned to wake up early anyway, because Ray had told me that the sunrise was spectacular in Logba Tota. I didn't want to miss it. I washed, dressed quickly and hurried to the front of the house with my camera at the ready.

I gazed at the sight that Anita Sinclair had been excited about. Rolling, undulating hills, no more than 3,000 feet above sea level, surrounded the area. The flora was amazing; the flat grassy valleys were lush. Birds chirped all around but I was unable to see them in the thick foliage. The hills had interesting, peculiar shapes and colonies of small villages nestled among them. Specks of rooftops peeked through the trees. I had travelled with a pair of binoculars and whipped it out to take a closer look. I saw movements. A dog barked in the distance and a car wound its way slowly along the narrow road. The villages were gradually coming alive. A shield of gray mist enveloped the valleys giving them a mystical appearance. As the first rays of sunlight descended upon them, like magic, the mist began to dissipate. Straight in front of where I stood on the paved front porch, the sun gently crested the mountain beyond, and as I gazed at it, a prism of light bounced off it. It was like a picture of heaven seen in religious storybooks.

A confusion of scents hit my nostrils. The scent of the land, plants, animals and flowers melded together with the early morning breeze and wafted through the air. Somehow Mount Sinai came to mind and I imagined Moses trodding up into a mountain similar to one towering in the distance before me, only to encounter the burning bush. As I gazed down over the misty valleys, and looked up at the brilliant sun fighting to shake the clouds, it all seemed so natural, so unspoiled, and so wonderful. I would have loved to remain in Logba Tota basking in its beauty for a month of two. Yes, Anita Sinclair was right – it seemed like almost heaven.

After breakfast, Ray led us on foot up a steep hill (Cars couldn't negotiate the grade.) into the village of Logba Tota.

The village broke my heart.

The thought that the place seemed like almost heaven vanished instantly. Having travelled a good cross-section of Ghana on my first visit, and having covered even more ground on this trip, I'd seen a lot. I'd seen wealth and poverty, but this was my first real face-to-face up-close encounter with life in a village. On our way up the hill, the first thing that caught my attention was the children. Several seven- and eight-year-old children, girls dressed in the standard brown tunics with peach blouses, boys in brown pants and peach shirts, were walking barefooted to school. They carried little wooden benches on their heads. They were taking their seats to school!

But it was the schoolhouse that caused me to gasp. It was a broken-down, dilapidated building with half of the red clay walls missing. The roof was lopsided and didn't fully cover the structure because walls to support it were not in place. There were no doors, just a gaping hole, and no windows. The ground surrounding the building was bare without a sprig of grass, just tough, clay-baked earth. Inside the structure was just as dismal. Small crude wooden desks were scattered about, and there were no chairs. That explained why the children travelled with their seats. A makeshift blackboard, held by a string, hung askew from a piece of wood attached to the top of one wall. Peabody and I looked at each other and our hearts went out to the people of Logba Tota, but more especially to the children, the next generation.

Sam, a young minister living in the area, and who was a part of Ray's church, had visited us after breakfast. He now accompanied us into the village. He led the way to his parents' home. We climbed over steep rock-face, up to the top of a hill where a few crumbling shacks (I couldn't call them houses.) stood. Many were duplicates of the schoolhouse with their broken down walls, missing walls, even missing roofs. Sam's parents greeted us in a narrow yard between their house and a large boulder. His mother was a teacher at the school with the missing walls we had passed on the way up the hill to the village. She was neatly dressed in western-styled clothes. The husband, much older, didn't say much. They offered us seats on wooden benches in the yard. A little boy, about three years old, took one look at Peabody, and with a big grin covering his face, rushed into her arms as if she was his long lost grandmother. Peabody was overwhelmed by the sheer joy on the boy's face. She hugged and kissed him. He clung to her as if he would never let her go. He remained on her lap until we were ready to move on.

Sam's parents lived in a small narrow house. I was itching to see inside and after talking with his mother for a while I decided to ask her.

"Mother, do you mind if I take a look inside your house?"

I watched her closely to see if I offended her but she was fine with it.

"Sure, come I'll show you," she said.

She opened the only door and led me inside. The house was basically one room divided into two by a white cloth screen. Four varnished wooden chairs were lined up against one wall. A small TV stood on a table straight ahead. She proudly pulled the cloth screen aside to reveal a double bed. The bed stood against one wall and a trunk was at the other end. There wasn't room for anything else. I wondered how she and her husband were able to get in and out of the bed. The approach could only be made sideways. The floor was made from rough unpolished wood. A small window carved out of one wall was opened. I looked out onto a thick tangle of bushes beyond.

I thanked her for showing me her home and we rejoined the others in the yard. It was obvious that Sam didn't live with his parents so I inquired where he lived. He showed me a small one-room house opposite his parent's home.

"Dat is my house. I build it to live in but we have storm one day and it blow off de whole roof."

"No kidding," I said, amazed by such an occurrence. Most of the houses with roofs had galvanized zinc ones. "So what did you do?"

Don't tell me he's living in the roofless house!

"I rent de house next door to my parents. Want to see?"

He gestured toward the door next to his parent's quarters. That was all the invitation I needed.

"Sure, if you don't mind."

I rose from the bench and followed Sam into his house. The room was similar to his parents' home. It had a small dining table, a double bed, and a small TV.

"It's not much, but I'm comfortable," Sam said.

Several thoughts raced through my mind. I wanted to ask him many things but I found it difficult to put the right words together to avoid offending him or appearing too inquisitive. So, I resisted and we rejoined the group in the yard.

Peabody and I had taken a keen interest in the plants in Africa and were always delighted when we recognized some we knew from Jamaica. We looked around the almost treeless yard and our eyes simultaneously caught sight of a familiar plant.

"Hey Peabody, look," I said pointing to a plant with large gray-green succulent leaves to the left of Sam's mothers house. "There's an oil nut tree! (*Ricinus communis*)"

"You're right, and look how healthy it is. There are bunches of seeds on it."

We were both excited. Sam's mother looked at us curiously.

"What is it?" she asked.

"We call it oil nut in Jamaica," Peabody said. "Castor oil is made from the seeds."

"I live here all this time and I see these plants all over but I didn't know the name," she said. "I didn't know you could make something from it."

Peabody took the opportunity to educate her on how castor oil is made, her big voice booming on the hill.

"When I was growing up in Jamaica my grandmother made her

own castor oil. Yvonne grew up with the same grandmother so she saw her making it too. You see those pods on the tree?"

"Yes I see them," Sam's mother said.

By now all eyes were focussed on the plant.

"When the pods are dry they open easily and all you have to do is remove the small dark seeds. You parch the seeds in a pot over the fire; then you pound them in a mortar. After pounding the seeds for a while, it becomes moist as the oil inside comes up. The next step, you put the pounded seeds in a pot with a little water to boil. You let it boil until the oil floats on top. You skim this off and boil it again. Grandmother used to call this process clarifying. A part of the mixture becomes like custard, similar to when you boil coconuts, and the rest is oil. It's a lovely honey-brown colour. You drain this and put it in glass jars. This is pure castor oil. We used it in our hair as pomade, and on our skin as lotion. After the summer holidays grandmother always gave us a dose of it as 'wash out' – a laxative."

"Please don't remind me!" I screwed my face to dramatize the disgusting taste of castor oil. "We would have the runs for at least two days after that."

Marie cracked up laughing.

"It's easy for you to laugh; you grew up under the clock; you have no idea what country living was like."

"Thank God," she said.

Peabody continued after the exchange. "We were never without castor oil at home. If you check out the drug stores you'll find all kinds of refined castor oils and you'll see it's included in all kinds of cosmetics. It's used in lubricants, paints and even dyes."

Sam's mother gazed at Peabody in awe. "Imagine this important tree is right here and I didn't know."

I was discovering as we journeyed throughout Ghana that the natives had little knowledge about many of the plants around them, and their uses. The potential to capitalize on them and make money was tremendous but the opportunities were lost.

We left Sam's parents and climbed down the rocks to visit the rest of the village. I had to slide on my derriere.

This place does not cater to old people, no ramps and elevators here!

Small one-room houses, similar to Sam's roofless house, were scattered around a central area. Like the schoolhouse, they were dilapidated, some without roofs. It seemed that no one bothered to rebuild or demolish and remove these houses. The middle area seemed like a meeting place. It was covered with a thatch roof but opened at the sides. A few benches and stools were placed there. The dirt was red and bare. A standpipe stood to one side and villagers were collecting water in various containers and taking it to their houses.

At this point something caught my attention and has remained indelible in my head. An old woman was cooking on an open fire on the ground. I assessed her to be about ninety. She was slim and bent. She managed to straighten up enough to look at me when I called out "Hello." She smiled at us, exposing toothless gums. She grabbed my arm and felt it, a strange behaviour. I thought instantly of the witch feeling Gretel's arm to see if she was fat enough. She spoke, but in dialect which I didn't understand. She was barefoot and wore raggedy clothes and a scarf around her head. Her small cast iron pot, black with soot, gurgled on the fire. The old woman bent over the fire and stuck her gnarled boney index finger into the boiling pot to test the food. I almost had a heart attack! Tears sprang to my eyes. Peabody watching my reaction, grabbed my hand and led me to the covered area where the elders had gathered and were speaking to Pastor Ray.

"How could this happen?" I asked Peabody, as tears rolled down my cheeks. "An old woman like that has no utensils; she has to put her finger in boiling water? Oh God, why?"

I was emotional and I knew Peabody was too, but she managed to control it better than I did. We'd both been raised by grandparents and had the highest regard for older folks. It ripped my heart out. What do you do when you witness such poverty and deprivation? A little money could help, but only for a few days. As I replayed the scene in my mind over and over, I became angry. What were the chiefs of the village, with all their pomp and ceremony, doing for people like these? Did they really care? Here were people living in one of the most beautiful places, with a landscape that was so enchanting, and yet their lives were deplorable. The poverty was carried on from one generation to the next with little change. I could already see the probability in the children. Did anyone in that village have any ideas about how to make life better and sustainable for these people? After witnessing that scene, I just wanted to leave. I felt too helpless, too riled up.

At a glance, Logba Tota seemed like almost heaven, but it was a living hell.

TWENTY ONE

TAFI ATOME

RAY WAS not aware of how Logba Tota had affected me and I took precautions to keep my sadness away from him. We left the village later that day.

Joe drove faster but carefully downhill, retracing our steps. As we turned onto the main road that would take us back to Tema, Ray turned to me in the back seat.

"Well Yvonne, what did you think?" He was smiling, satisfied with the trip because besides showing us around, he'd been able to discuss business with the elders of the village regarding upcoming events and services.

"There is no doubt about it, Ray, the place is beautiful." It was the truth; the view was beautiful but the living was ugly. I lied by omission by not stating how I felt about the poverty and destitution of the villagers. "I'll always remember Logba Tota. Thanks for taking us to see it."

"You're welcome. Not far from here is a place called Tafi Atome; it's a monkey sanctuary. We'll stop there for a little while."

"Do we get to see some monkeys?" Marie asked a redundant question, but as it turned out, it wasn't redundant after all.

"I can't guarantee you that you'll see monkeys. They are wild, not caged, so they're in the bushes. I think they like to play games and hide from humans. It depends on the mood they're in and how long you want to wait."

Monkeys are always fun creatures to watch, in a zoo anyway. I thought it would lift my spirits.

"Oh Ray, you have such great ideas. I would love to see the monkeys.

You know, while we were in Kumasi, we wanted to visit the animal reserve in the north at Tamale. We'd hoped it would be our version of a mini safari but our host discouraged us from going there."

"Really? Why?"

"She said it was too dangerous to go there without an escort. She was really scared for us."

"I don't know much about up there, but maybe she was right."

We settled back into Joe's car and enjoyed the scenery. Soon we arrived at Tafi Atome where we entered the Visitor Centre and paid a small fee. Six white tourists – a middle-aged couple and two young couples – were ahead of us. The young ladies were dressed in cut-off jeans and sleeveless tops with bare shoulders. How inappropriate, I thought. They were about to enter a forest not knowing what kinds of insects and bugs they would encounter, yet they were exposing so much skin, tempting faith. The middle-aged couple dressed more appropriately in slacks and cotton shirts. Our group was dressed with little skin exposed. We congregated at the counter and a guide gave us a brief history about the area.

"About 300 monkeys live in this forest. They are the endangered True Mona Monkeys. When the ancestors arrived here about 200 years ago, they protected the monkeys because they believed they were messengers to the gods. In the late 1980s, because many of the villagers were Christianized, they lost their faith in the monkeys. They tried to prove that they didn't fear the monkeys any longer and killed some of them."

A sympathetic "Oooh" went up from the group.

I'd mentioned before that sometimes I'm not sure if the way the natives were Christianized was always a good thing. This was a perfect example of the downside to the process. Imagine killing God's creatures to prove that you believed in God and you weren't afraid.

"The people also destroyed a part of the forest. But some of the villagers realized that even if the monkeys were not as reverent as they had believed, they could be good for tourism. They joined with NGOs and created this sanctuary in 1993. Since that time the forest and the monkeys are protected."

The guide left us to walk about on our own. A plaque engraved with some information stood at one side of the room. I walked over and read the inscription.

At Tafi Atome, a village 43 kilometres south of Hohoe is the Monkey Sanctuary. The monkeys at the sanctuary are believed to

have protected them from calamities throughout their exodus from Assin in the Central Region to their present abode. According to Togbega Adza Kodadza 1V, Chief of Tafi Traditional Area, anyone who dared to challenge the mystical powers of the monkeys fell sick or died. He said no one had ever seen a dead monkey in the area.

Lack of knowledge can lead people to have strange beliefs and to do bizarre things. Zoology teaches that the monkeys buried their dead. Mystical powers had nothing to do with the absence of dead True Mona Monkeys.

"I feel as if I'm walking on holy ground," I whispered to Peabody.

"You better take off your shoes from off your feet," she retorted.

We both laughed and dashed outside to join Ray, Marie and our driver and tried to keep pace with the rest of the group. We trekked into the forest for some time, following a slight track on the ground. It was obviously made from all the traffic of tourists and natives looking for the animals. It had rained earlier making the air damp, but the soil beneath the canopy was fairly dry. The rain hadn't penetrated the thick foliage. We kept looking up into the trees, hoping to spot some of the endangered species; however, we found no monkeys. I felt cheated, ripped off. But there was no point being angry; Ray had warned us of the possibility. We began to retrace our steps when a boy about twelve came rushing into the forest.

"We found some, come dis way," he shouted.

"Are you sure?" the middle-aged woman asked.

I understood the reasoning behind the question. We'd travelled some distance into the forest; we didn't want to waste time going further to no avail.

"Yes, we saw some, Ma'am."

We followed the lad with quickened pace. He was right. In an area where the forest had thinned out, four monkeys scampered proudly up in the trees. They were obviously aware of our presence and put on a show for us. They chattered and swung from branch to branch. They were incredible. Two were medium-sized and two were babies. I'd never seen the True Mona Monkey species in any zoo. These four were either black or gray with a white apron down the front from their chins, making them look like little old men with white beards. A ring of white, resembling a hat, encircled their heads. Their big eyes gave them a unique appearance. The largest one had a reddish tinge in its coat. We all scrambled to take pictures of the monkeys as they frolicked.

Satisfied that we had seen what we hoped to see, Ray suggested that we'd better get moving. On the way back to the car my cousins and I thanked him for stopping to allow us to see the beautiful creatures. There was a good possibility that we would never see that species again.

TWENTY TWO

RETURN TO ACCRA

On our way back from Logba Tota, Ray asked the driver to take us directly to Accra, Ghana's capital. Except when we had arrived there, my cousins and I hadn't yet spent anytime in the city. Upon Ray's instructions, the driver took us straight to the Kwame Nkrumah Memorial Park and Mausoleum.

My mind quickly filled up with fond memories of Adamson and the time he took me to the site. I recalled that day clearly: On a hot, sunny day, just before noon, Adamson drove his car slowly up the path, allowing me to savour the moment. The park had a well-manicured lawn, pruned trees and exotic flowers. Colourful butterflies flitted from one pollen-filled flower to another while birds chirped from the trees. The mausoleum was a futuristic-looking structure made from variegated gray granite. In front of it stood a larger-than-life statue of Nkrumah, Ghana's first Prime Minister after the country gained independence from Britain. In front of the monument was a dual fountain with two rows of statues depicting atenteben players, crouched on pedestals. Crystal clear water cascaded over the fountain. I anticipated the thrill of seeing the place again.

We wound our way up the path and parked nearby in a designated area. Looking over the statue, Marie and Peabody seemed impressed. But something was missing; something wasn't quite right. The statue of Nkrumah and the atenteben players didn't look the same. Then it dawned on me; someone had painted the bold black statues with gold paint. It took away much of the dramatic effect. Besides the addition of the gold paint, the upkeep of the park had deteriorated. Vendors with unsightly booths now sold food and drink on the premises; I was disappointed. Peabody and Marie had nothing to compare; they appreciated their visit inside the mausoleum and the information about Nkrumah.

The second stop was the crafts market. Marie, our shopping queen, was in her element and geared up to buy. There were rows and rows of stalls with colourful clothing, beautiful materials, carvings of every description, beads and an array of other items, all made in Ghana. We stopped at a booth and the three of us purchased Ghanaian outfits. There were no fitting rooms to try them on. We used our best judgment coupled with Ray's input. Once we did that, the competition among the vendors for our business became so intense, we had to hurry out of the market.

"Whew!" Peabody said. "I thought a fight was going to break out."

"Everyone wants to sell you something," Ray said.

"Well, they certainly ruined it for themselves. I would've bought more stuff but I couldn't stand the pressure."

"So sorry, you have to forgive them," Ray said in his soft African-flavoured voice.

Two boys about twelve years old had been trailing us from the moment we entered the street. They followed us to the car and pleaded with us to buy from them. Ray took charge of the matter.

"Okay guys, let us see what you have."

They opened two vinyl bags and displayed several flat wooden carvings, the type you hang on walls. Marie was interested. She held up a carving of a woman with a basket of fruits in her hands and a baby at her back, wrapped tightly in the mother's clothing.

"Oh mommy, look. Isn't this adorable?"

"It's nice," Peabody replied.

The carvings were different from many we'd seen in the market. While the faces and limbs of the women depicted were made from dark wood, the dresses and headgear were in colour. Marie and I purchased two pairs each. The boys were extremely happy, and thanked us several times.

The driver then took us on a sightseeing tour of the town. During the tour, Ray pointed out interesting architectures and government buildings.

TWENTY THREE

BOOKS FOR FRIEDA

I SPRANG OUT of bed to the barking of dogs, the crowing of roosters and the gentle swish, swish of a broom on parched dry dirt. It was my last day in Ghana. These sounds will resonate with me for a long time.

The first morning after I arrived in Tema, while lying in bed, I heard a swishing sound. Curious to know what created it, I had opened the louvre window and looked out onto the yard immediately behind the townhouse. An old woman who lived in the house behind our abode was bent over, using a short broom made from twigs without leaves to sweep the yard of baked hard dirt. I'd marvelled that in the 21st century, some Ghanaians were unaware or couldn't afford a simple tool such as a broom with proper fibre and a handle. From that day, without fail, the sweeping occurred at the crack of dawn every morning.

I raced to the bathroom before everyone to shower and to fix my hair. Afterwards, I placed my towel and washcloth on the wall of the enclosed porch. The daytime temperatures of 32 degrees Celsius would have them bone dry within an hour, ready to be packed into a compartment of my suitcase.

Later I joined the two pastors and my cousins at the breakfast table. Tension in the air was so thick; you could chop it with a cleaver. Alma the maid, who'd become quite attached to us, didn't hum as before. She plodded through the house as if she'd lost a sibling. She seemed sadder than Afua in Kumasi, but at least Afua had a tangible reason to be sad. Breakfast was a solemn affair. It began with a passionate prayer by John. Alma served us without the customary bright smile and avoided making eye contact.

"At this time tomorrow you'll be back in your country," John said, looking at the cousins across the table.

"Not quite," I said. "I'll be back in my country, but Peabody and Marie will be spending a few days with me before returning to the United States.

John grinned, exposing his *Chiclets*. "You're right; I keep forgetting that Canada and the USA are two separate countries."

"You're not the only one to do that. I met a minister in Nigerian a few years ago and he made the same mistake. He had been trying to visit the United States for years and finally made it the year after my trip. He telephoned from New York, wanting to visit me. When I told him that he had to go to the Consulate General of Canada to obtain a visa, he couldn't understand why. I took pains to explain that Canada is a separate country with its own Prime Minister and currency and that he couldn't just cross the border without a visa."

"Well that much I know," John said.

"Don't laugh, he was an intelligent man. He told me that the media in Nigeria always referred to Canada and the United States together so he assumed they operated like one country."

Ray changed the subject. "How's the packing coming along ladies?"

"We practically lived out of our suitcases, so we only have a few things, mainly the stuff we bought, to pack," Peabody said.

"I just hope my suitcase can hold everything," Marie said, her voice filled with doubt.

I'd given away several items and felt confident that my suitcase would accommodate everything.

Once we finished breakfast, John retired to his room, probably to prepare for service the next day, although I suspected that was not the only reason. Peabody and Marie returned to the bedroom to clean up and to finish their packing.

The middle-aged man, who washed clothes for the household, always sat on a small bench just outside the back door. I never saw him enter the house, but I always chatted with him from the open door. Today he was not in the mood to talk.

Ray, wanting to get away from the melancholic atmosphere, had other ideas. He came and sat beside me in the living room. He began to stroke my arm.

"Yvonne, I know you said you wanted to spend some more time

with Frieda before you leave; I just thought of something."

I looked into his clear brown eyes and he looked away bashfully. "What did you have in mind?"

"There's a ship that comes into the harbour every year at this time; kind of a floating bookstore. I was thinking of taking you and Frieda on the ship and we could look around. I want to buy some books anyway and their prices are much better than the shops here. They also have a good variety."

Our eyes met and held this time.

"That is a great idea, Ray. I could buy some books for Frieda, too. When should we go?"

"I think now is a good time. We could spend about three hours."

"Three hours will be perfect."

Our flight to Amsterdam was scheduled for 6 p.m. and we had to be at the airport at least three hours before departure. I had at least three hours to spare. I dashed upstairs to fetch my handbag and to tell Peabody and Marie about my plans.

Ray and I left the house together and walked out to the main road where he hailed a cab. We stopped to collect Frieda at her aunt's house. Unaware of our plan, Frieda came to the gate when Ray knocked on it. He spoke to her briefly and from where I sat in the back of the cab I could see a wide grin spread across her face. She dashed back into the house and reappeared shortly, wearing a blue dress, running shoes and carrying her new knapsack. Ray opened the back door of the car for her and she slipped onto the seat beside me. She gave me a big hug. I'd taken her shopping the previous day and had bought her a new school bag, shoes and socks. The shyness seen earlier had slowly disappeared; now we were great friends.

"Hello auntie," Frieda said, her face brighter than the morning sun.

"Hello Frieda, did Ray tell you where we're going?"

"Yes Ma'am, he said on a ship."

"That's right. Have you ever been on a ship?"

"No Ma'am."

"I guess this will be an adventure then?"

"Yes Ma'am."

Ray directed the driver and we drove leisurely toward Tema's harbour. Taxis weren't allowed to enter the wharf; the driver deposited us at the gate. We walked for a long time, passing large metal containers, boxes, crates, barrels and all kinds of heavy equipment. Ray held my hand on one side and Frieda's on the other and together we strolled about the harbour like a happy little family. I still didn't understand the handholding, but I refrained from reading anything romantic into it. We passed a group of youths walking along the wharf. Many seemed to know Ray; they called out his name.

"Gee Ray, you have your own fan club here," I said.

"Oh, some of them come to church; some are in our youth groups."

By this time it was mid-morning and the heat was intense. Sweat began to stream down my face. Poor Frieda, wearing her new knapsack, shifted it from one side to the other, no doubt wishing that we would arrive at our destination as soon as possible. Thank goodness I'd worn running shoes and not fancy sandals.

Finally I saw it. A grey majestic structure, several stories high, loomed out of the ocean, imploring us to come on board. Security was tight. We joined a long queue of students, teachers and parents waiting to get on. The ship's personnel were allowing only a certain number of people on at a time. Thirty minutes later, long-legged Ray bounded up steep narrow steps with Frieda following close behind. I brought up the rear, barely able to catch my breath. I felt as if I'd just completed the marathon. A friendly female student directed us where to go and we entered a huge room. Stacked wall-to-wall with books, the room was like a gigantic bookstore warehouse. Books were arranged on shelves, some spread out on low stands with clear labelling, which made it easy for patrons to find any genre they wanted.

Frieda went crazy like a toddler opening presents on Christmas morning. She moved from aisle to aisle, shelf to shelf, touching books, opening some, looking at pictures in others.

"I never see so many books in my life!" she said, grinning like Garfield the cat.

"Do you have any favourite stories you like to read?" I asked.

She stared it me with a blank look on her face.

"What kinds of books do you like to read?"

"I don't know," she said, looking down.

"Do you have any books of your own?"

"No Auntie, only school books."

This is unbelievable.

Here in the 21st century is a young lady of 12, heading into her teenage years, who has never owned her own storybook. My mind flashed back to when I had been her age and attending high school. My grandparents who raised me had been poor, but I was able to purchase at least a few books besides textbooks. I was an avid reader during those days, and the ones I couldn't buy were borrowed from my more affluent classmates. The "hot" books then were Nancy Drew, Hardy Boys, and the Bobbsey Twins. We were going through puberty and curiosity was raging. Besides these mystery books, we had experienced the world of romance vicariously through Mills & Boon romance novels. Books provided our entertainment.

All of my classmates were reading these books and many of us could not afford to buy them. The deal therefore was: you could borrow from those who owned but the books had to be passed on within three days. Many were the nights when I stayed up until 1 a.m. reading by lamplight, determined to finish a book. Looking back at those days, I think that I was fortunate; the situation instilled in me the desire to read. It also taught me to take care of books because those precious publications had to be returned to their owners for lending to other classmates.

"Have you ever heard of the Nancy Drew and Hardy Boys stories?" I asked my protégée.

Another blank stare. "No Auntie."

"Okay then, I think I'll buy you a few. You need to read books, not just textbooks." I turned to Ray. "I'm going to take her to the teen's section."

"All right, I'm going over to the theology area; let's meet back at the cashier in say, 40 minutes?"

"That should do it. Let's synchronize our watches."

We did. Ray headed off to religion while Frieda and I embarked on a treasure hunt. It didn't take us long to find Nancy Drew and Hardy Boys books. Frieda flipped through pages of a few of them and agreed that they looked interesting. I picked out four books and handed them to her.

"I'll buy these for you."

"Oh thank you, Auntie, thank you."

I wanted to capture the thrill on her face as she held the glossy new books; it was priceless. Unfortunately, I hadn't brought my camera with me.

On our shopping spree the previous day I'd asked Frieda what she would like to be when she grew up. "A journalist," she said without hesitation. This made it all the more important for her to begin to read widely. We walked along the aisles, looking to see if anything else caught our attention. I spotted a shelf of literary aids.

"You know Frieda, there's an important book that you should have. Do you have any idea which one it is?"

She looked at me with big bright eyes, and smiled with confidence. "A Bible? I have one already."

I looked at her standing in the aisle, pretty and slender, with her boyish haircut. She looked more wistful than Mona Lisa.

"Well young lady, that is an important book and I'm glad to hear that you have one, but for your education, you need another 'Bible' – you need a dictionary."

I'm not quite sure that she got the gist of that statement; however, I picked out an Oxford dictionary for her. It would be the most important purchase as far as I was concerned. We walked over to the cashier near the front where we'd entered. I paid for the books and handed them to her. Right away she put them in her knapsack.

"I want you to use the dictionary at all times," I said. "Look up every new word you hear or read. You said you want to be a journalist; well it is a valuable tool for journalists."

Innocent eyes gazed up at me and I prayed that the message was absorbed. She gave me a hug and thanked me again.

Ray was standing just beyond the cashiers' station when we arrived there. He held a small stack of books in his arms. He moved over to join us. It had gotten very hot on board the ship; my throat was parched.

"Do they have a coffee shop or snack bar on board for patrons?" I asked Ray.

"Oh yeah, I was going to suggest we get some refreshments."

He steered us toward a deck with a covered snack bar. Listed on the menu were hot dogs, burgers, cakes and several flavours of ice cream among other items.

"How about some ice cream?" I asked Frieda.

"Yes, Auntie. Can I have a hot dog, too?"

"Of course, whatever you like. Would you like the same Ray?"

"Sure. Chocolate ice cream for me."

"What about you Frieda? What's your favourite flavour?"

"Vanilla."

I ordered ice cream cones and hot dogs for us. We collected our food from the server and walked over to the side of the ship. We ate our dogs, licked our cones, and gazed at the huge harbour and azure ocean. Disturbing thoughts seeped into my mind. Within hours I would no longer see Ray or Frieda. I pushed the thoughts aside.

Frieda beamed like a beacon all the way back home. When we parted, she promised to read the books and to take care of them. We would continue to send e-mails from across the Atlantic.

At the townhouse, Pastor John gathered together the entire household, including Alma. He prayed for the safe journey of the travellers back to Canada. We hugged him and thanked him for his warm hospitality. He mentioned that he had pressing matters to attend to and retired to his room.

Peabody and Marie drove in a taxi with Alma, who insisted on going to the airport to see us off. Ray and I sat in the back seat of another taxi that was loaded with most of our luggage. As the taxis wound their way to Kotoko Airport, Ray held my hand as if it were a precious object.

"Yvonne, I can't tell you how much it has meant to have met you," he said.

"The pleasure has been all mine, Ray. You and John have been hospitable, kind and superb hosts. Thank you so much for all you've done and continue to do for Frieda."

Ray turned to look directly into my eyes, his face morose and thoughtful. "There's so much I want to say; I don't know where to begin."

I patted his hand. "It's all right; no need to say anything. I just wish for you everything that's good and wonderful. I hope you'll find the 'western woman' that you want so much."

He leaned over and kissed me on the cheek. "Be blessed, Yvonne; be blessed."

INDEX

A

Accra 154
Ackee 129
Adamson 9, 10, 11, 12, 13, 14, 15, 20, 22, 32, 42, 54, 96, 97, 140, 154
Africa 11, 14, 21, 37, 38, 41, 43, 55, 85, 97, 147
Africa Gin 130
Akwaba 24, 35, 38, 95
Akwasi 41, 42, 43, 44, 48, 49, 53, 54, 55, 57, 58, 59, 63, 64, 65, 66, 67, 69, 71, 117
ancestors 3, 13, 16, 17, 37, 47, 63, 80, 86, 127, 151
Asantehane 59
Asantehene 61
Ashanti 50
awestruck 31, 56

B

baguettes 129
banana 30
banku 97
bauxite 31
Belcacgek 33, 34
Benin 122, 136
Bible 18, 68, 161
Blue Cheese 79, 88
books 7, 50, 107, 158, 159, 160, 161, 162
bootleg 130
Bosumtwi 55, 56
bougainvilleas 34
breadfruit 31
Breadfruit 31
Burkina Faso 119

C

cacao 104
camaraderie 39, 118
canons 79
Canopy Walkway 3, 6, 77
Cape Coast 82
Cassava fish 27
Castor oil 147
cedar 30
Chief 68, 69, 152
Christianity 30, 41, 52
Christianized 68, 105, 151
CityAccra 29, 42, 84, 96, 162
CityKumasi 3, 29, 40, 43, 119
CityplaceKumasi 25
CityStateAccra 22
CityToronto 35, 77
claustrophobic 83
coconut 30, 55, 58, 105
coffin 33
continent 15, 16, 17, 29, 37, 44, 117
country-regionAshanti 42, 45, 54, 62
country-regionBrazil 86
country-regionBurkina Faso 43
country-regionCanada 42, 44, 55, 157
country-regionGhana 11, 13, 15, 16, 19, 27, 31, 41, 44, 55, 117, 119, 121, 129, 154
country-regionJamaica 16, 105, 126, 147
country-regionMali 43
country-regionNigeria 157
country-regionplaceTogo 126
country-regionSierra Leone 94
country-regionTogo 105, 117, 120, 121, 126, 129, 136
country-regionUnited States 44, 58, 121, 144, 157

D

death 10, 15, 20, 24, 38, 39, 40, 41, 47, 48, 49, 58, 71
diabetes 17, 45
Diaspora 84
dilapidated 33, 58
DOOR OF NO RETURN 83
drill sergeant 86
dungeons 80, 83, 84
duplex 38, 39, 70

E

effigies 60
Efutu 91, 114
Elmina 3, 77, 78, 84, 93
Europeans 29, 30, 43, 84
Ewe tribe 122

F

Fanti 79
female urinal 72
fishermen 80, 142
fishmongers 116
flora 8, 72, 144
flowers 31, 32, 34, 67, 75, 94, 123, 145, 154
frangipani 34
French 31, 117, 127, 134, 136
Frieda 20, 21, 99, 100, 101, 102, 108, 109, 110, 111, 112, 113, 114, 115, 139, 156, 158, 159, 160, 161, 162
fufu 14, 33, 45, 97, 118
funk 82, 83

G

garri 118
Ghana 1, 24, 45, 97, 154
Gold Coast 43, 57, 61
Golden Stool 59, 61
grasscutter 32, 33
Gulf of Guinea 119

H

Hans Cottage Botel 90, 91
harbour 86, 104, 115, 116, 142, 158, 161
Hotel De La Paix 123
Hotmail 101

I

incarceration 81

J

jackfruit 128, 129
Jamaica 5, 47
jolloff rice 97

K

Karite 54
kenkey 97
Kente 45
Kingdom Hall 105, 106, 110, 114
King Prempeh 61
Koby's Hotel 25, 26, 95, 99, 102, 104, 117
Kofi Annan 45, 46, 93
Koforidua 29
Kotoka 23
Krobo tribe 100
Kumasi 61
Kwame Nkrumah 57, 154

L

lizard 27, 28, 79
Logba Tota 139, 141, 143, 144, 145, 146, 149, 150, 154
Lome 122, 124
Lomé 133

M

Maroons 62
mausoleum 154, 155
melancholy 48

meteor 56, 57
Middle Passage 86
Mona Monkeys 151, 152
Motherland 20
mourners 48, 49
Muslims 14
Mystical 152

N

Nana Yaa Asantewaa 61
Nanny 62
natives 30, 120, 126, 127, 137, 142, 148, 151, 152
Ninenight 48

O

Obuasi 57, 58
Otumfuo Opoku Ware 11 59, 60
Otumfuo Osei Tuti 59

P

palm wine 127, 128, 129, 130, 131
Paloma 95, 96, 97
Pastor John 103, 106, 107, 108, 109, 110, 111, 112, 113, 117, 139, 141, 162
Pastor Ray 21, 22, 44, 98, 99, 101, 102, 103, 104, 106, 111, 112, 149
phenomena 55
placeAfrica 3, 10, 11, 14, 15, 16, 17, 18, 20, 23, 29, 31, 35, 37, 41, 44, 73, 87, 94, 103, 115, 117, 119, 124, 126, 127, 129, 130, 131, 132, 136, 142, 157
placeAtlantic Ocean 80, 85, 115, 124, 136
placeCityAccra 25, 26, 29, 36, 93, 94, 95, 96, 104, 141, 154
placeCityKumasi 14, 25, 26, 28, 29, 33, 34, 38, 39, 42, 43, 45, 48, 54, 59, 61, 63, 67, 70, 71, 116, 118, 151, 156
placeCityNiagara Falls 126, 132
placeCityToronto 11, 19, 20, 40, 68
placecountry-regionAshanti 13, 16, 24, 31, 37, 38, 40, 44, 46, 47, 48, 51, 53, 55, 56, 59, 60, 61, 62, 70, 71, 117, 119, 127
placecountry-regionBenin 105, 124, 134, 135, 136, 137
placecountry-regionBritain 16, 29, 57, 154
placecountry-regionCanada 11, 12, 19, 21, 35, 58, 85, 89, 109, 110, 121, 127, 157, 162
placecountry-regionGhana 3, 10, 12, 18, 19, 21, 22, 23, 24, 27, 29, 30, 31, 32, 33, 34, 40, 42, 43, 45, 46, 52, 53, 54, 56, 57, 59, 63, 66, 68, 72, 77, 79, 80, 81, 82, 84, 87, 91, 92, 93, 94, 95, 96, 98, 99, 100, 102, 104, 105, 112, 118, 119, 120, 126, 127, 128, 129, 130, 137, 139, 141, 142, 145, 148, 155, 156
placecountry-regionJamaica 6, 13, 16, 31, 40, 54, 58, 60, 62, 65, 129, 147
placecountry-regionMali 15, 19, 41, 42, 43, 44, 117
placecountry-regionNigeria 13, 27, 67, 96, 117, 129, 144
placecountry-regionSierra Leone 18
placecountry-regionTogo 44, 117, 120, 121, 122, 124, 126, 127, 129, 133, 135, 137, 138, 139, 141
placecountry-regionUnited States 16, 42, 43, 86, 94, 112, 114, 157
PlaceNameKakum PlaceTypeNational Park 3
PlaceNameMfantsipin PlaceType-School 93
PlaceNameVolta PlaceTypeRiver 141
placePlaceNameKakum PlaceTypeNational Park 3, 4, 93

placePlaceNameManhyia PlaceTypePalace 59
placePlaceNameMfantsipim PlaceTypeSchool 92
placePlaceNameMfantsipin PlaceTypeSchool 92
placePlaceNameSlave PlaceTypeCastle 77, 78, 79
placePlaceNameVolta PlaceTypeRiver 119, 137, 141
placePlaceTypeCape PlaceTypeCoast 3, 4, 63, 70, 72, 73, 75, 77, 78, 79, 84, 85, 86, 88, 89, 91, 93
PlaceTypeCape PlaceTypeCoast 3, 77, 78, 79, 89
placeWest Africa 14, 85
platform 8, 9, 111, 115, 121
Poinciana 67
Prempheh 1 60
protégée 21, 99, 160

Q

Queen Mother 50, 51, 61
Quobna Ottobah Cugoano 83

R

rain forest 1, 4, 5, 8, 10, 142
roosters 53, 144, 156

S

Savanna 117
Schiphol 22, 23, 102
Shea 54
slavery 80, 85
spathodea 94
stench 82, 83
sterling 16

T

Tafi Atome 150, 151
Tema 21, 44, 98, 99, 102, 103, 104, 105, 107, 109, 115, 117, 121, 122, 138, 139, 141, 150, 156, 158
tilapia 97, 136
Tilapia 57
Togo 122, 136, 137
Togolese 124, 129, 134
traditional 32, 46, 50, 60, 91, 97
tunic 30
Twi 57, 92, 106

U

uniforms 30, 54, 58, 92, 121
United States 5

V

vegetation 30, 31, 55, 92, 104, 117, 126, 132, 142
villages 30, 57, 72

W

wake 48, 114
waterfall 126, 131
West Africa 17

BURKINA FASO
BENIN
GHANA
Bolgatanga
Gushiago
Yendi
Tamale
Bole
Bimbila
TOGO
Salaga
IVORY COAST
Lake Volta
Sunyani
Mampong
ASHANTI REGION
Kumasi
Ho
Obuasi
Koforidua
Volta
ACCRA
Tema
Winneba
Cape Coast
Takoradi
GULF OF GUINEA
50 km
50 miles

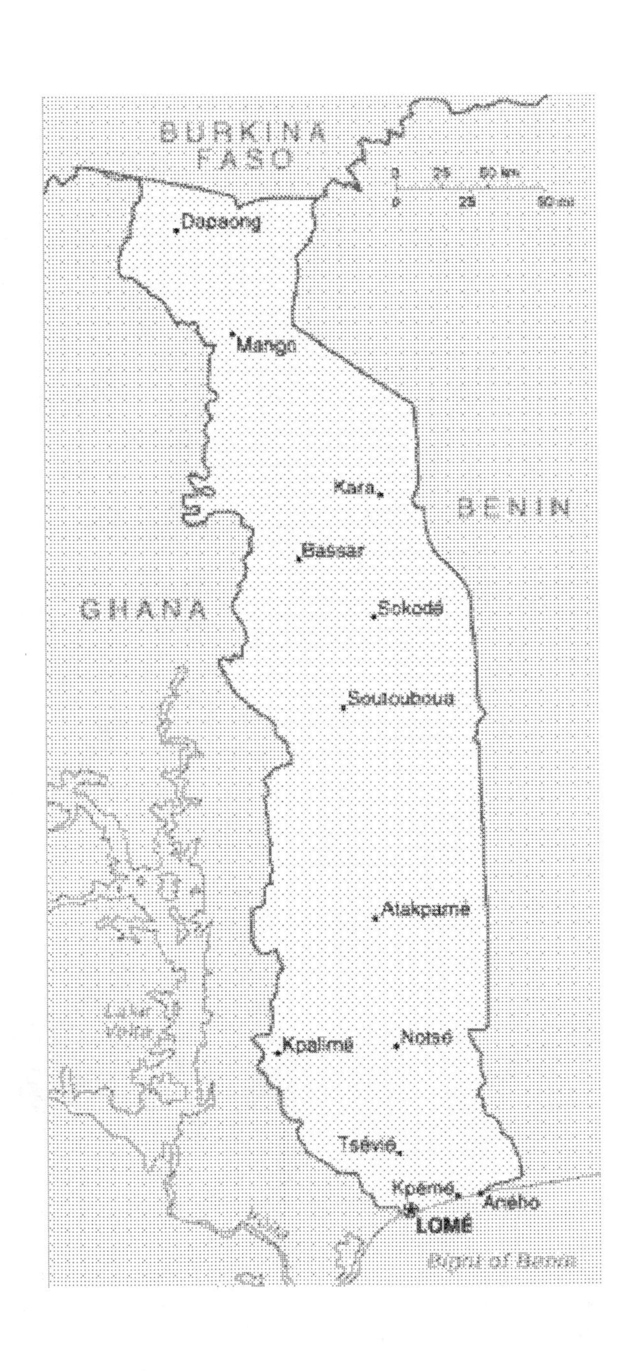
BURKINA FASO
0 25 50 km
0 25 50 mi
Dapaong
Mango
Kara
BENIN
Bassar
GHANA
Sokodé
Soutouboua
Atakpamé
Kpalimé
Notsé
Tsévié
Kpémé
Aného
LOMÉ